INVIN

WRITTEN BY SALLY ROSENBERG ROMANSKY

ILLUSTRATED BY MARGOT JANET OTT

AFTERWORD BY CHRISTOPHER REEVE FOUNDATION

imagination stage

Published by   Imagination Stage, Inc.
                4908 Auburn Avenue
                Bethesda, Maryland 20814
                www.imaginationstage.org

Library of Congress Control Number 2006920163
Library of Congress Cataloging in Publication Data
Romansky, Sally Rosenberg

Invincible/Sally Rosenberg Romansky; Illustrated by Margot Janet Ott

ISBN 0-9723729-4-6
1. Juvenile Fiction   2. Animals—Horses   3. Social Issues—Special Needs

Printed in the United States of America by HBP, Inc. 2006

Text illustrations done in watercolor and ink; Cover illustration done in watercolor and pastel.

Dedication

To the Kessler family, and particularly to
Isabel and Olivia, who inspire and model a
world of acceptance,
courage and genuine mutual love...

To my dad, Harry, and my late mom, Francine,
whose infectious appetites for learning, personal growth,
and nurturing deep and enduring relationships
inspire me daily to be a better
parent, wife, daughter, friend, and writer...

And

To my husband, Mike, and our children,
who believe in me and who, through their
love and support, provided me an environment
within which I could create *Invincible*.

Chapter 1

"Finally I'm getting out of this castle!" Princess Lena rejoiced. "Tell me you're excited, too, Meg."

"Of course!" said Lena's identical twin.

"I wonder which horses will pull our coach. I can't believe I'll be close to horses!"

Meg smiled.

"And, maybe we'll finally make some friends!" Lena said.

"Lena—just because we're going to the village doesn't mean Mother and Father suddenly will change all of the rules."

"Mother and Father won't be able to keep me from making friends. I *can* talk."

"Please, don't get your hopes up."

"Where is Fran? Aren't we supposed to be getting ready?"

"She'll be here. She won't make us late."

"What could she be doing? Let's go find her."

Meg went to the doorway and peered out. She looked up and down the long corridor. Sun rays beamed through windows that lined the full length of the hall. Meg squinted. No sign of Fran.

"Let's go to her room," said Lena.

No point in telling Lena to be patient, Meg thought.

Fran's bedroom door was slightly ajar. Lena leaned forward and pushed it wide open. Fran was crouched over her desk, examining a document. Upon seeing the princesses, she hurriedly folded the paper and tucked it into her skirt pocket.

"Birthday girls!" Fran darted to the door. "I was just on my way to get you ready for your special outing."

"I couldn't wait any longer," Lena said. "Don't you think ten years is long enough?"

"Oh, Lena." Fran placed her hand under Lena's chin. "I know you're excited. Still, you can't leave until the appointed hour."

"I want to get ready...please, can you come, please?"

Fran smiled. She escorted the girls back to their room. Out of their armoire she removed two silk lavender gowns with crystal beads decorating the scooped necklines and dotting the full-length sleeves.

"Fran, I've never seen those!" said Meg.

"Your mother had them made specially for today."

Meg clapped her hands. "They really look like dresses princesses would wear!"

"That's because you are princesses!" said Fran.

"Who finally get to show the world who we are!" Lena said.

Fran dressed the girls, one at a time. They took turns having their long hair brushed and braided.

"Now, for the finishing touch—tiaras!" Fran said.

"Tiaras! Finally we have a reason to wear them!" Meg said.

Fran walked to the glass case that hung on the wall. Meg rushed to her side. Fran opened the glass doors and removed one shimmering headband.

"May I hold it?" Meg asked.

"Carefully," Fran said. Meg eyed the diamonds and emeralds on her headpiece, then lifted it. "Fran, will you crown me Princess Meg?"

"With pleasure." Fran took the tiara and raised it high. Meg giggled. Fran lowered it slowly atop Meg's braids and securely positioned the gem-studded band.

"My lady," Fran curtsied.

"Now, mine!" Lena said.

Fran fixed Lena's jeweled headband and curtsied before her as well.

"All the villagers will bow and curtsy to you today," Fran said.

"You're sure they know we're coming?"

"Quite sure, Lena. Your parents must have sent a dozen messengers to announce your presentation today."

"And they'll want to see us, won't they?"

"Of course, Lena, dear. I imagine they've wanted to see you since you were born. It's been ten years of waiting for them, too."

"Ten years too many!"

Fran kissed each girl on the forehead. "I'll let your parents know that you are ready. You are the loveliest ladies in the land."

"I wish Fran were going with us," Meg sighed.

"There's no room in the coach, remember?"

"I know. I just would like her to be with us."

"Did you see what she was looking at when we got to her room?" Lena asked.

"No."

"You didn't notice anything?"

"No, I didn't."

"Well, she was leaning over her desk, looking at some paper. Couldn't you tell she was startled when she saw us? And she folded the paper so quickly. And she stuffed it in her pocket. Don't you wonder what it was?"

"Surely nothing that matters to us." Meg turned her head. "I think I hear footsteps." She lifted her skirt and shuffled to the door. She looked down the hall.

"They're coming! It's Mother and Father!" Meg said.

"Finally! Let's go!" Lena said.

Chapter 2

"We're so proud—so proud to introduce you," the King said. The King sat next to the Queen in the coach, across from their daughters.

"Are you all right?" the Queen asked, directing her question to Lena. "Are you comfortable?"

"Yes. Fine," Lena replied.

The King squeezed the Queen's hand. "Today, once again, we give thanks for our beautiful daughters. And, today, we are blessed to have you accompany us!"

"Tell us again, Father. How will you pass out the gold coins?" Meg asked.

"Twenty soldiers will ride in front of us. Each carries a bag of gold. As they have done every year on your birthday since the day you were born, they will present a coin to each villager who greets our procession. This is one way we show thanks for having you as our daughters."

"It's so romantic!" Meg sighed.

Lena had no patience for the tale. "Can we leave? Isn't it time?" she asked.

The King nodded. He tapped the wall behind him and the coach wheels began to turn.

"I wish I could see the horses," Lena said. "What are their names?"

"I believe Sir and Ruby are leading us today," the King replied.

"Can't I pet them when we get out?" Lena pleaded.

The King turned to the Queen. She shook her head no.

"Mother!" Lena protested. "It's my birthday. Petting the horses would be a perfect gift!"

"Lena—please." The Queen leaned forward to touch Lena's knee. "Please. Let's not ruin this special day. You know we don't want you near the horses—you might get hurt. Please."

Lena frowned at her mother. She'll see, Lena thought. I'll do more than touch a horse one day. I'll ride one.

Meg reached for her sister's hand. "Let's enjoy the ride, okay?"

Lena nodded. "How long a ride is it?" asked Lena.

"Usually about an hour," said the King. "Enjoy the countryside girls! It's time you saw how lovely this part of our kingdom is."

The girls turned to gaze out the coach's windows. The cobblestone path that led from the castle rapidly turned into a narrow dirt path, bordered with broad oak trees and wildflowers in deep gold, scarlet and purple. The girls' wide eyes darted everywhere. After ten minutes, Meg noticed a cluster of trees with skinny white trunks.

"What are those trees, Father?" Meg asked.

"Those are white birch."

"I must remember exactly what they look like so I can paint them. The trunks look as if they are made of snow!"

The coach rocked from side to side as it rattled down the narrow lane.

Lena worked hard to keep her balance. But, Meg was seated so close to her that she didn't have far to fall if she toppled. Lena stretched toward the window, seeking wind on her face.

She had been asking to join her parents on this journey for as long as she could remember. Whenever her father and mother took a trip, she had begged to join them. But, she pleaded extra hard on her birthday. It seemed particularly unfair that her parents went to town every year to give thanks for her birth, but left her behind.

"When you turn ten," her mother had promised on her eighth birthday.

"Why wait until we're ten?" Lena had protested. "Why can't we go now?"

"That's when you will become young ladies," her mother had explained.

That made no sense to Lena. "I might go crazy waiting until then," Lena had replied.

"You'll manage," her mother had said with a smile.

Since then, Lena had lived for this day. She imagined the children of the village gathering around her, asking her what it was like to live in the castle. She would tell them about the canopy beds and lavender baths, the tiaras and the servants. But, then she would ask them to tell about their lives. That's what she wanted to know—what it was like to be a regular child, who got to go to school and play with friends. And then they would agree to be friends. And to visit one another. They would come to the castle and she would go to the village.

It was going to be wonderful—and it began today, with this trip.

The coach rumbled along the narrow path flanked by thick woods. Soon, the trees thinned and farms began appearing. Lena and Meg recognized grapevines, apple and peach trees, berry bushes and cornfields. The castle grounds were dotted with vineyards, orchards and vegetable fields, so these sights were not new. The barns and stables they saw sliding past the coach windows looked like the royal barns and stables the princesses could see from their bedroom window. The one-story houses reminded Meg of some of the servants' quarters.

But, when the road turned from dirt path to a cobblestone road once again, everything looked different. On either side of the coach were small buildings lining the road. Each was labeled with a carved wooden sign above the doorframe. "Bakery," "Apothecary," "Tavern," "Dry Goods."

"The village! We're here!" Meg called out.

"Where is everyone?" Lena asked, straining to see out the window. "Why is no one here?"

"They are waiting for us in the village square," said the King. "That is where we will stop the coach."

"And, that's where we will get out? And meet them?" Lena felt somersaults in her stomach. This was it—what she'd waited for.

The King and Queen looked at one another and then back to Lena. "Your father will be getting out, Lena. No one else," said the Queen.

Lena felt as if the air had been sucked out of her lungs. She stared at her mother's face; it might as well have been the face of a statue. There was no hint that the Queen was joking.

Chapter 3

"We are not getting out of the coach today," the Queen said. "We will see everyone through the windows."

"But, you've told us how you get out and greet the villagers every year!" Lena said.

"I know. But, this year is different. Your father will greet the crowd alone," the Queen said.

"Why?" Lena's face was turning fiery red. "Why can't we get out, too?"

"We thought it would be best for the rest of us to stay in the coach," the Queen answered.

Lena's left hand began to twitch. "Why?" she demanded.

"We thought we should take it slowly—it being the first time," the Queen said.

"Take what slowly?" Lena shot back.

"You know very well," the Queen said.

"No, I don't," Lena said. "I don't at all."

The Queen looked to the King, as if she wanted assistance. He gazed at the coach floor.

"It's just…it's just…," the Queen stammered. "We don't want you to get hurt."

"Hurt? Doing what? Meeting people? How could we possibly get hurt?" Lena cried.

"Something could happen, Lena," the Queen said.

"Like what?"

"You could be knocked over. The villagers could trample you," said the Queen.

"With Father holding me? With the guards surrounding us? Impossible!" Lena protested.

"Lena, please, we're almost there. This is how it's going to be," the Queen said.

"You don't want them to see me up close, do you? You're embarrassed by me!"

The King raised his eyes to look at Lena. "We're not embarrassed by you, Lena. Never. Never think that," he said.

"Well, you've caged me in all these years. Every ball you ever have hosted—Meg and I have had to watch from the balcony. Every visitor you've ever entertained has been a mystery to me. I thought you finally were letting me out. But, you're not!"

"Lena—calm down. Do you want them to see you so agitated? We're almost there. You *will* see them. You're just not getting out. It will be too involved to get you out and we don't want them rushing up to you. Truly, you might get hurt," the Queen said.

"That's what you say all the time. I might get hurt!" Lena pressed her fists into her lap. "I won't get hurt! I won't!"

"We can't be too careful, Lena," the Queen said.

"But you are too careful!"

"Lena," the King interjected.

"I want to meet the villagers! I want to make some friends," Lena insisted.

The King rubbed his hands together over and again. "Lena, I thought you knew how today would work."

"Well, I didn't. I didn't at all. I should never have come. Take me back! I'm not a circus animal. Take me back!"

Meg reached over to her twin.

Lena latched on to Meg's hand. "I'm sorry, Meg. I know you want to go…but, I don't anymore. I can't!" Tears rolled down Lena's cheeks. "Take me back, please."

Meg's stomach knotted as it always did when Lena was upset. Meg kneaded her middle with her free hand, trying to loosen the tension.

"Let's go back." Meg's voice quivered.

"No," the Queen said. "That is not an option. It is our duty to complete this journey! Besides, they can already see us approaching!"

"It's not fair to Lena," Meg said.

"Fair has nothing to do with this," the Queen stated. "We will continue this journey. We will present you as planned. We will not disappoint our subjects. And, Lena, you will look stately and proud, as will Meg. Dry your tears."

"Seeing the people and not being able to be with them will only make me feel worse," Lena said.

Her mother frowned. "I'm sorry," she said. "I wanted this day to please you. Now, wipe those tears away. Look like the proud princesses you are."

"You'd let Meg get out if I weren't here. Wouldn't you?"

The Queen was silent.

"Wouldn't you?" Lena glared at her mother.

"Nonsense," the Queen finally said.

"Father?" Lena's eyes pleaded more than her voice. She wished that once, just once, he would admit that her mother was wrong to keep her cooped up. The King always urged Lena to be patient—he kept saying that her mother would come around. After all, he had said, they were going to the village on the birthday ride this year. Well, Lena would rather have stayed home than have to stay in the coach. Lena was tired of waiting—she needed her father to overrule her mother. Maybe he would do that, finally, right now. He *was* the King.

"Father?" Lena asked again.

The King sighed. "Lena, do your best to enjoy yourself. You've waited for this day for so long."

Lena's face hardened. She stared out the window, her thoughts racing. Why can't he ever stand up to her? I'll have to break free on my own. Meg and Fran will help me.

The coach came to a halt. The girls saw the King's soldiers standing in a semicircle around the coach, facing a crowd. The villagers were at such a distance, the girls could barely make out their faces. They could see rows of children in the front, standing on tiptoes, stretching to get a glimpse of them.

"Lena—look—all the villagers are here," the Queen said.

Lena scoffed. "We can't even see them. They're just a bunch of bodies squished together. And they can't really even see us. Isn't that what you wanted, Mother?"

"Please try to enjoy this moment, Lena," the Queen begged.

Suddenly, a trumpet sounded.

"Announcing his majesty, the King!"

At once, the princesses saw the mass of bodies bow and curtsy. The little bodies in front stumbled and fumbled to keep their balance.

A soldier approached the coach and swung the door open. A few villagers craned their necks, trying to see inside.

Meg felt Lena's hand still twitching in hers. Meg couldn't wait to get home.

The King emerged to a silent crowd. He lifted his arms high into the air and his subjects stood at attention.

"I thank you for greeting us on this most special day," he called. "We celebrate another year in the lives of our sweet princesses, Lena and Meg. And, today, we have the great joy of them accompanying us on this blessed journey. We know that you each have loved ones in your lives. May you celebrate them today as we celebrate our beloveds."

The King twirled his robe and reentered the coach. The crowd cheered.

The King tapped on the wall of the coach and the driver snapped his reins. Sir and Ruby clip-clopped and led the coach around the perimeter of the semi-circle made by the villagers. The King and Queen began to wave, and motioned for their daughters to do the same. Lena saw the villagers stretch and twist, hoping to catch a glimpse of the coach's occupants.

I want to see you too, Lena thought, as she waved. And I will. I'll work harder than ever to get stronger. And, then, I'll be back. And it won't be in this awful coach. I'll be back riding Sir or Ruby or some other horse. I will. I will.

Chapter Four

The King emerged from the coach and beckoned to Fran. His face was long.

"What's wrong?" Fran asked. "What happened?"

"Lena thought we would be getting out of the coach in the village—to greet the villagers personally. When she learned that we didn't want her to get out, she became so distraught. It was awful. Please fetch her chair."

Fran ran to get the wheeled chair and rolled it on its gilded wheels to the carriage. The King stepped into the coach, lifted Meg down and set her on the path. Meg's head hung low. Fran went to her and pulled her close. Meg's body was limp in Fran's embrace.

"Help, Lena," Meg said. She started shuffling toward the castle, unmindful of her birthday gown. The long skirt dragged in the dust.

The King took Lena from the coach and gently lowered her onto the satin cushion that padded the seat of her chair.

"You're ruining my life." Lena's eyes challenged her father.

"That breaks my heart," the King said. "We just want to protect you. We worry about you so."

"You let Mother's worries decide everything! You know I can do so much more than she allows. She probably knows that, too. She just doesn't want anyone to see me. It would make her look bad, I guess."

"Lena, that's enough. Don't talk disrespectfully of your mother. Your mother is not embarrassed by you," the King said.

"Fran, run Lena a nice lavender bath. See if that won't help settle her down," the Queen instructed, peering from the carriage.

"Settle her down," Lena mimicked. "That's all you want is to settle me down. You've never thought I could do anything. You said I could never sit up by myself. But you were wrong. I can. I learned how. And you wanted Fran to keep feeding me. I told you I could learn to feed myself. To use a fork. To raise a glass to my lips. And I did. Didn't I?"

"Come, Lena. Come. We'll talk." Fran turned the chair and began pushing it toward the castle.

But, Lena wasn't through. "You're wrong about me, Mother. I'll show you again and again that you are wrong," she called back over her shoulder.

"Lena—my darling. I know you've wanted this day for so long," Fran said. "What happened?"

"It was the worst day of my life."

By the time they arrived at the princesses' room, Meg had already shed her silky dress. It lay in a heap on the bed.

She crossed the room to her sister and knelt by her, taking Lena's hand in hers. "I wish this day had been different."

"Didn't *you* think we were getting out of the carriage? Why go if we couldn't get out?"

"I hadn't really thought about it. I just wanted to go. To be part of the procession. To see what the village looked like. I didn't need to meet everyone. I just wanted to see it."

"That was enough for you? Just to see it?"

"It would have been. But, after what happened, I couldn't wait to leave." Meg rose and walked over to her armoire. "I want to go paint."

She slipped into a paint-splattered smock and walked out the door.

Fran went to draw the bath the Queen had ordered.

"Mother thinks a bath is the answer to every problem," Lena said. She stared out the window which ran the full width of the room. Lena insisted that the curtains be open always. She watched the sunrise each day and imagined all the lands the sun greeted. Lands she planned to see someday. And she could see the horse stables and barns in the distance. For now, *that* was the only place she really wanted to go.

Horses pulled the coach that took her parents to other lands. Horses brought messengers who delivered news from other Kingdoms. Horses pulled the plows through the fields beyond the royal gardens. Horses were transportation. Horses were strong. For as long as she could remember, horses captivated her. They could take her all the places she longed to see. She wasn't sure *how* to make it happen, but she was determined. And she didn't want to wait any longer. If her parents wouldn't let her out into the world, then she would get out on her own.

"Fran," Lena called, "we're going to do some new muscle work. I need to get stronger—quickly."

Fran returned.

"Why?" she asked as she pulled off Lena's slippers.

"Mother won't let me do anything. She won't let me go any-where. I embarrass her," said Lena, as Fran continued to undress her.

"I don't believe that, Lena," Fran said. "Your mother is just scared. She's been afraid for your safety ever since we noticed that you couldn't move your body the way Meg could. You were eight months old and still not sitting up. Meg had been sitting up for two months by then, and was starting to crawl. She also was holding her own spoon and cup by then. You couldn't grip anything securely. And then, Meg started to walk, but you—you were still squirming on your back and flailing your arms and legs without any semblance of control. Your mother was terrified, Lena. She was scared then, and she's scared now."

"But, Fran, she didn't want the villagers to see me. Like, that's what she was afraid of—not that I could have been hurt. How could I have been hurt?"

"Maybe she didn't want your *feelings* hurt."

"What do you mean?"

"She may be concerned that other children will tease you— or even be afraid of you."

"Because I can't walk?"

"People can be cruel, Lena. When they see someone who's different, sometimes they say mean things. Sometimes they get frightened."

"But, it's not like I can help how I am. I was born this way."

"I know…but, sometimes, when people see others who look different…they pull away…because…I don't know…maybe they fear that they could become that way, too. So, they run away or tease the one who makes them uncomfortable. Yes, I think they get scared."

"We're not scared of Mr. Stuts—and he looks different!" Lena said.

"You and Meg know how to look beyond how someone appears," Fran said. "Not everyone is like you two."

Lena stared out the window.

"So, you're saying that the village children wouldn't want to be friends with me…because I can't walk?"

"That's possible, Lena. That's quite possible."

Lena couldn't believe what she was hearing...she couldn't believe that this was what her mother was trying to protect her from.

"I think it's Mother who's afraid of being teased. Teased that she has a damaged daughter!"

Fran shook her head. "You mustn't think that, Lena. You mustn't. Your mother has been grateful for you since the moment you were born."

But, Lena did not believe her.

"Well, I think I *could* make friends. I'll show Mother and Father. I'll prove to them that people will want to be friends with me," Lena said. "Fran—I need to get stronger. I need to be able to ride a horse, so I can go somewhere—everywhere!"

"Learning to ride a horse...Lena, that's a long way off. But, you know that I'll always help you to get stronger," Fran comforted. "Always."

Fran hung up the princesses' dresses and lifted the determined girl in her arms like a baby. Lena's arms dangled at Fran's side. Her right hand scraped against what felt like a piece of paper sticking out of Fran's skirt. Lena swung her hand away from it, and saw it drop. She almost told Fran to pick it up. Then, she remembered the paper that Fran had stuffed so hurriedly in her pocket that morning.

No, Lena thought, I won't tell Fran about the paper. I'll look at it first. And I'll find out what Fran was trying to hide.

Chapter Five

Lena's toes wiggled under the covers as Fran said her good-nights. For once, Lena didn't want to stretch out Fran's bed-time ritual. She wanted Fran to leave—as soon as possible—and she prayed Fran wouldn't notice her mysterious paper on the floor.

Lena had managed to kick the paper most of the way under the bed earlier in the day when Fran wheeled her past it on their way to meet Meg. Controlling her legs well enough to do that was something Lena had only recently accomplished. Lena knew that, at some point, Fran would realize the paper was missing—and Lena wanted a look at it before then.

"Tomorrow will be a better day," Fran said, kissing the girls' foreheads.

"We'll do my new exercises, right?" Lena asked.

"Of course," Fran smiled. She bent to blow out the candles next to the bed.

"Please leave them," Lena said. "I'd like to read."

"Be careful putting them out," Fran said, directing her attention to Meg.

Meg nodded.

As soon as Fran left, Lena poked Meg.

"Quick, hop out of bed!" Lena said. "You'll see a paper on the floor, sticking out at the foot of the bed. Grab it and bring it here!"

"A paper?" Meg asked.

"Yes. It fell out of Fran's pocket. I think it's what she was looking at in her room this morning. Let's see what it is!"

"Why don't I just pick it up and take it to Fran? It is hers."

"Meg, please! I managed to keep her from seeing she had dropped it. I just want to peak at it."

"Lena, that's snooping."

"It's not snooping when it's in our room. We're doing her a favor really—finding it for her. Please, Meg, get it—and we'll just see what it is."

Meg slipped out of bed, crouched, lifted the bed skirt, and saw a folded paper lying on the ground. "Here it is," she said. "I'm taking it to Fran."

"Meg, wait! If we don't look at it, we might never know what's on it!"

"Which seems to be what Fran wants."

"But, Meg, maybe it's something we should know about. Maybe it's a letter from someone in her family. We might finally find out something about her real family."

Meg considered this possibility. Suddenly, she became concerned. "Oh no! What if it's a letter asking her to come home?"

"Exactly," Lena said. "We would need to know that. So we could stop her."

Meg stared at the paper in her hands.

"Come here! Open it!" Lena said.

Meg hesitated. "I don't want Fran to get mad at us."

"We'll give it back," Lena said.

Meg studied the paper. "Actually, I think it's kind of old. Look—it's yellowish. And it has deep creases—like it's been folded and opened many times."

"Maybe it's an old letter then—maybe a love letter?"

"You think Fran has a secret love?"

"Maybe."

"Lena—you don't think Fran would ever leave us, do you?"

"If that paper has something on it that tells us Fran is thinking of leaving us, we need to know—right?"

Meg nodded.

"Unfold it, Meg—come on," Lena pleaded. "Or, give it to me. I'll do it."

"It might tear. I'll do it," Meg said. She carefully unfolded the worn paper.

"It's a drawing!" Meg said.

"Show me!"

Meg hopped back into bed and planted herself next to Lena.

Lena guided Meg's hands so the paper was spread across the coverlet. Her eyes darted across the page.

"I think it's a map!"

"Of what?" Meg asked.

"Who knows? All these squiggly lines must be roads or paths. And these look like trees," she said, tracing the odd shapes with a fingertip as she continued to scan the paper.

"There's a purple wax seal down here—can you move the candle close?" Meg did. "It's some kind of weird symbol. Like a cylinder or something—see?"

Meg ran her finger over the seal. "I don't know what that is."

Lena continued to study the map. "Look!" she said. "The only other color on the whole map is this blue oval..." Lena tilted the page. "It's hard to see in this candlelight, but it looks glittery—see?"

Meg nodded. "It shimmers, at least in this light." She pointed to some faint marks near the blue patch.

"Are those letters?" she asked.

Lena squinted. "I think so! Get the magnifier!"

Meg slid out of bed and retrieved the magnifying glass from their bookshelf. She held it over the glistening blue oval.

"I need more light—can you hold the candle nearer?"

Meg obliged.

"That's good!" Lena said. "I can read it! It says 'Palindrome Pond.' That's a funny name. And, there's more." Lena's eyes strained to read the small print. "It says, 'Are we not drawn onward, we few, drawn onward to new era?'"

"What could *that* mean?" Meg asked.

"I have no idea—but it seems there's a place called Palindrome Pond."

Lena paused. "I wonder where it is." She studied the map again. "Look, Meg—in the corner here—it looks like a castle."

"I see," Meg said. "You're right. It is a castle. But, it's not the same as the rest of the drawing. The ink looks newer, and the style is different. Whoever drew it didn't draw the rest of the map. I think it was added later."

"Thank goodness you're an artist, Meg. I never would have known that!"

The girls huddled together, eyeing the map carefully.

"Meg, you should draw a copy of this map. Then, we can give this one back to Fran but still have one of our own to study."

Intrigued in spite of herself, Meg agreed. "Best I do that in the daylight," she said.

"But Fran may come looking for this soon. I think you need to draw it now."

"I can try—but I can't promise I'll see every detail."

"Well, try, and don't forget to write down those words about the new era. Quick! In case Fran comes looking."

Meg took the paper to a table near the window, set the candle down, and speedily began to sketch.

Chapter Six

"Isn't it fun to have a mystery to solve?" Lena asked as Meg wheeled her through the long stone corridors to the library.

"I have to admit—yes, it is," Meg said as she shoved open the library's heavy door.

Light flickered from dozens of candles set upon reading tables scattered around the room. Sunshine barely penetrated the dark, stained-glass windows designed to keep the sun from fading the books.

Meg and Lena were frequent visitors here. Lena especially loved to discover new books. When she read, she pretended to be part of other worlds, other lives.

Meg wheeled Lena into the main room.

"Let's look in the map cabinet," Lena suggested. "Maybe we can find a more detailed map that will give us a better idea where Palindrome Pond is."

Meg wheeled Lena in front of a wide wooden cabinet that had at least three dozen thin drawers.

"How are these organized?" Meg asked.

"I don't know. Open a drawer and see what's in there."

Meg pulled open a drawer. "There's a stack of maps in here." Meg flipped through them. "They have titles on the top—Section 100, Section 101, Section 102. This isn't any help. We'll have to look at every single one—and there must be at least thirty in this one drawer. If we want to find a map to Palindrome Pond, we'll have to ask Mr. Stuts."

"Let's not get him yet," Lena said, thinking hard. "Why don't we look at the books about people's lives?"

"You mean the biographies?" Meg asked.

"Yes. Maybe Palindrome was a famous person," Lena said.

Meg guided Lena's chair across the room to a bookcase labeled "Biographies" in gold script at the top. Mr. Stuts had organized the books alphabetically by the last name of the person they were about. So, Meg searched the shelves until she found the "P's."

"Paffley...Patterson...Penzance...Pildro," Meg said. "No one here named Palindrome."

"Hmm," Lena mused. "Now what?"

"How about Mr. Stuts' *Book of Words*?" Meg suggested. "Maybe it's just a word."

"Okay!" Lena agreed.

Meg relocated Lena to the shelves marked "Reference" and lifted the heavy *Book of Words* onto a neighboring table. She flipped the pages.

"'P-A-L-I-N-D-R-O-M-E'—it's here!" Meg said.

"What does it say? Read it!" Lena cried, squirming in her chair.

"'A word, phrase, verse or sentence which reads the same backward or forward.'"

"How do you read something backwards?" Lena asked.

"There are some examples here."

"Like what?"

"'Tot' or did' or a phrase like 'never odd or even'."

"I don't get it. I see that 'tot' is 't-o-t' and 'did' is 'd-I-d' so it reads the same whether you start at the beginning or end. But, if you read 'never odd or even' backwards, you get 'even or odd never.' How does that phrase read the same backwards as forwards?"

"That's not what it means by backwards," Meg said. "Reading backwards is starting from the right side instead of the left!"

Meg moved the book so Lena could see it. "Look," she said. She traced her fingers from the right side of the phrase "never odd or even" to the left. "See, it does still say 'never odd or even', just the spacing isn't right."

Lena studied the words. "Oh! I see!" She traced her fingers along the letters from right to left and saw "neve ro ddo reven."

"How fun!" Lena said. "I bet we could think of lots of palindromes! Like 'pop' or 'bib'."

"Or 'toot'" Meg said.

"Coming up with phrases is harder." Lena narrowed her eyes as she tried to think of a palindrome phrase. "I don't know if I can do that!"

Meg concentrated. "I see what you mean," Meg said. "Single palindrome words are pretty easy to think of. Like, 'pup' or 'noon'. I think we'd need pen and paper to come up with a palindrome phrase."

"But," Lena wondered, "what could this have to do with a pond?"

"Can a pond look the same from one direction as it does from the other?" Meg asked.

"I suppose," Lena said. "Maybe its bank is exactly the same all around it?"

Meg pictured the map she had copied. "Lena," she said, "those words on the map—the ones about the new era..."

"Yes?"

"Do you think those make up a palindrome phrase?"

"You have Fran's map, right?"

"Yes, right here."

Meg pulled the paper out of her pocket. She gently unfolded it and took a magnifier from the reference shelf. "'Are we not drawn onward, we few, drawn onward to new era?'"

"Now, start reading from the right—does it say the same thing?" "'are wen ot drawno nward, wef, ew, drawno nward, ton ew erA!' Incredible!" Meg said. "Just like with 'never odd or even'. The letters aren't grouped into the words properly—but, yes! It is the same!"

"See," Lena said, "I told you there was a mystery here!"

"What does 'era' mean?" Meg asked.

"I don't know. Look it up!"

Meg flipped to the "e's." "'Era—a period of time that is notable because of its new or different events, aspects or personages.'"

"So—'new era', it's like a new time, or something like that," Lena thought aloud. "It's time we find Mr. Stuts. He'll help us learn more. Maybe he even knows about the pond."

"He must be down one of the tunnels," Meg said. She shivered. "Those tunnels spook me."

"I know," Lena said, "But, we have to find him! Let's try the History Tunnel first. Didn't Mr. Stuts say that he has been working on some project reorganizing the history books about the pharaohs of Egypt?"

Meg pushed Lena through the aisles until they reached a wall of books interrupted by a wooden door with the word "History" carved above a metal grating. Shadows cast by torchlight flickered through the grate.

Meg hesitated. "Can't we wait until he comes out?"

"No. Fran will be here soon to get me for my exercises. Come on! You know nothing's in there except books!"

Meg slowly turned the knob and pulled open the door. She returned to the back of Lena's chair and pushed her forward.

The ceiling arched above them. Books lined both sides of the tunnel, leaving little room for Lena's chair. Torches were mounted in brackets every few feet, encased by glass covers to ensure the books were shielded from the flames.

Meg coughed. "It's so cobwebby and creepy. How can Mr. Stuts spend so much time in here?"

"You know how he loves books. Just like me," Lena said. "I'll call him. Mr. Stuts! Mr. Stuts, are you down here?" Her voice echoed off the ceiling and down the tunnel.

No answer.

"Let's go down a bit further," Lena instructed.

"Maybe try a different tunnel."

"Not yet. I really think he's down here. Come on, a bit farther."

Meg obliged.

"Mr. Stuts!" Lena cried out.

"Lena," a faint voice traveled to the girls.

Lena bounced up and down in her chair. "See, he's here! I knew he would be! We can go back to the big room and wait for him there."

"Good," Meg sighed, retreating up the tunnel.

The girls waited at the mouth of the tunnel until they finally heard Mr. Stuts' uneven steps.

The old librarian emerged, blinking in the bright light of the main room. He bowed.

His uncombed white hair hung from just above his ears all the way down his back. It tumbled forward with his bow. He lifted his head, exposing an odd countenance. His left eye was slightly farther from his nose than the right, and his lips were stretched out farther left as well. He wore a higher heel on his left shoe to try to even his shorter left leg with his longer right leg—but he still walked with a limp.

"How I can help you today my young Highnesses? Do you want suggestions for new books?"

"We're here to solve a mystery!" Lena blurted.

"A mystery, eh? My favorite! Tell me!"

"We're trying to find out about Palindrome Pond? Do you know of it?" Lena asked.

Mr. Stuts' bushy eyebrows twitched. His nose twitched. His mouth twitched.

He was silent for a moment. "How did you hear of such a place?"

Lena looked at Meg. The princesses had agreed that if they asked for Mr. Stuts' help, they would not tell him about Fran's map. They didn't want him telling Fran they had it. And, Fran might not want him to know about it either.

"We saw it written somewhere," Lena said, trying to sound casual. "Do you know of it?"

Mr. Stuts' eyes veered to Meg, then back to Lena. He stroked his hair in a rhythmic up-and-down motion, as he always did when he was deep in thought.

"Have you found any clues?" he finally asked.

"We couldn't figure out how to look through the map cabinet. We didn't find any biography about someone named Palindrome. So, we looked up 'palindrome' in your *Book of Words*," Lena said, "and we found out that a palindrome is something that reads the same way backwards and forwards. There must be some reason a place is called 'Palindrome Pond.' Don't you think?"

"Indeed," replied Mr. Stuts, still pulling on his hair as if he were milking a cow.

"Well," Lena said, "can you give us another clue? Is there anything we can read about palindromes? There must be something more than the definition you wrote."

"I think I can oblige," he said. "I'll be back."

Mr. Stuts limped past the princesses to the door marked "Philosophy" and disappeared. His uneven step sounded once again.

He emerged with a thin book, blowing dust off its cover. He handed it to Lena.

"*Palindrome Discourse,*" she read aloud.

Just then, Fran appeared.

"Why, hello Mr. Stuts. You have a new book for the girls?"

"The princesses are trying to solve a mystery."

"That sounds fun," Fran said.

"The mystery," Mr. Stuts continued, speaking slowly and sounding out each word precisely, "is what and where is Palindrome Pond?"

He eyed Fran.

She returned his gaze.

Lena watched Fran closely. Surely, Fran now knew that the girls had found her map. Fran didn't flinch. Lena couldn't tell if she was upset, or even concerned.

"And this book?" Fran asked.

"I have given them an essay about palindromes. Perhaps it contains a clue."

"I see," Fran said. "Well—may they take it with them? It's time for Lena to exercise."

"Indeed," Mr. Stuts bowed.

Chapter Seven

"So, you found my map?" Fran asked as they entered the sunroom.

"Here it is," Meg handed the paper to Fran. "We were careful with it." She studied Fran's face. "Are you mad?" Meg asked.

"No, not mad exactly," Fran said. "Curious, I suppose. Why didn't you come to me with it? Why Mr. Stuts?"

"We just wanted to have a little adventure—that's all," Lena said. "A mystery to solve."

"Still, it's my property," Fran said. "You should have come to me."

"We didn't show the map to Mr. Stuts," Meg assured. "We didn't tell anyone about it."

"Okay," Fran touched Meg's cheek.

"What new exercises have you thought up?" Fran asked Lena.

"Is that it? You're not going to tell us anything about Palindrome Pond?"

"I hadn't planned to," Fran replied.

"Are you going there?" Meg asked. "Are you leaving us?"

"Never. I would never, ever leave you. You are my family," Fran said.

"Do our parents know about Palindrome Pond?" Lena asked.

"Not that I know of," Fran said. "I haven't spoken to them of it…"

"Why not?" Meg asked.

"Well, it's kind of a secret," Fran said.

"A secret you won't tell us?" Lena asked.

"One day, perhaps. But, not now." Fran said.

"You sound like Mother," Lena complained. "Everything that I want will happen one day."

"I know it's hard to wait, Lena, but, wait you will. Some things are better learned when we are older. In the meantime, you have the book Mr. Stuts gave you—that's a good start."

"If we have questions after we read the book—will you answer them?" Lena asked.

"Perhaps," Fran said. "Now, weren't you determined to build your muscles stronger? Are you so distracted you've forgotten that?"

"Never," Lena said. "I've got a great idea. You know how I sit with my back to the wall, bend my legs and push an empty crate out over and again?"

"Of course," Fran said.

"Well, now I want you to start adding books to the crate to make it heavier. Don't you think that will help my legs get stronger?"

Fran smiled. "I do."

"Didn't you once tell me that to ride a horse your legs need to be able to press against his belly when you want him to move?"

"Well—it's one way to let a horse know that you want him to move. There are other ways—like using the reins or making certain sounds."

"Still, it would be good if my legs got stronger, right?

"Of course. Your legs also would have to be able to stretch apart wider to fit across a horse's back."

"So, I'll need to work on stretching, too."

"Indeed," Fran replied. "But, let's be clear. I've no plans to put you on a horse—certainly not anytime soon."

"I know…but, the stronger I get, the closer I'll be to riding," Lena said. "True?"

"True," Fran said.

Meg reached for some books from the bookcase.

"Are you going to help me?" Lena asked. "It's okay if you paint instead."

"I want to help," Meg said. "I want to see how much weight you can push."

Fran lifted Lena and set her against the wall. Meg dragged the wooden crate from where they kept it next to the bookcase and positioned it near Lena.

"How many books to start?" Meg asked.

"Let's try four," Lena decided. "Big ones."

Meg placed four hardcover books in the crate. She placed the crate a short distance from her sister as Fran helped Lena to bend her legs.

"You may never be strong enough for me to stand on," Lena said looking at her legs, "but, you will keep me on a horse one day—you will."

"You're reminding me of when you talked your hands into being steady enough to hold a glass," Meg said.

"And I spilled hundreds of glasses before I could do it," Lena said.

"Right—but, then you did it," Meg said.

"And I'll try this thousands of times if I have to," Lena said. "Because I will do it. I need to. I've got to get on a horse."

"Let's just focus on getting you stronger," said Fran.

Meg moved the crate forward and Fran positioned Lena's feet so that her soles were flat against it.

"Push, Lena," Meg said.

Lena braced her body with her hands on the floor next to her. Her legs wobbled. She focused her eyes on her feet pressing against the crate. She inhaled deeply. As she breathed out, she pressed her legs forward and moved the crate a tiny bit. She breathed in again and pressed her feet in rhythm with her exhale. The crate edged slightly farther away.

Lena looked into Meg's encouraging eyes, then took another deep breath and pushed again.

The crate didn't budge, though Lena was straining as hard as she could.

Lena looked at Meg again, so frustrated she wanted to cry.

"Let me take most of the books out," Meg said. "Then try."

Lena nodded.

Meg removed three books.

Lena tried again.

This time, she moved the crate far enough to straighten her legs.

Chapter Eight

"Hooray!" the King's deep voice boomed from the doorway. "My beautiful girls," the King entered. "My pride in you grows daily." He bent to embrace Meg, then Lena.

"Girls, it's time your mother and I leave for Prince Frederick's wedding," he said.

Usually, Lena would beg to join them. And, as always, her parents would say no. But, this time, Lena was content to stay home and work on gaining strength.

"How long will you be gone?" Meg asked.

"Two weeks," the King replied. "The journey to the Prince's land is quite far." The King gave Meg a squeeze. "We will stay in touch by messenger, of course." Then, he turned to Lena.

"I'm glad to see you are back to your work. I hope this means your spirits are improved from your birthday."

"No. I'm still mad about that. You should have let us meet the villagers," Lena replied.

"You must understand that your safety is what matters to us above all. As you get older, and grow stronger, you will get to do more."

"You can't keep me cooped up here forever! I'll find a way out."

"Lena, give it time. This year, we took you to the village. That was the beginning."

"Well, not the kind of beginning that made any sense. I could have gotten out of the coach and talked to the villagers— you know that."

"Lena, your mother feels strongly that it's too soon for that."

"Why? Because she actually thinks I might get hurt? Or because she doesn't want the villagers to see her damaged daughter."

"Lena, you're not damaged!" the King said.

"That's what Mother thinks, doesn't she?"

"No, Lena, that's just not so."

"So, what is it then?" Lena asked. "Fran says Mother may be worried that other kids will tease me—say mean things, run away from me."

"That's true, Lena," the King said.

"Shouldn't it be up to me? What if I want to try?" Lena asked.

"Lena, you may think you can handle more than you can," the King said.

"Do you really think they would tease a princess?" said Lena.

"Lena, I love you with all my heart and soul. You'll never know how hard it is for parents to know what to do when a child isn't well."

"I am well. I just can't walk or move my body perfectly like you can."

"We are doing our best. Everything we do is out of love for you. Everything."

"Then, let me go to the horse stables!"

The King stared at his daughter. He took a deep breath and wrung his hands.

It looks like he's thinking about it, Lena thought. He actually looks like he's thinking about it. Lena forced herself to remain silent—to just look at her father with pleading eyes.

"Come with me," he said, scooping her into his arms.

"To the stables?" Lena asked, hoping that it was true.

"Not quite, but it will be a first step," he said.

Lena smiled.

"Meg, do you want to come along?" the King asked.

"To where?" Meg said.

"Just outside—to where the horses are standing at the gate," the King said.

Meg hesitated. "No thanks," she said. "I'll watch you from up here—from the balcony."

The King strode outside, Lena's arms tight around his neck.

He stopped just outside the main gate where a knight on horseback was stationed on either side.

"Which horse would you prefer to pet?" the King asked.

Lena's smile widened. "The white one, I think!"

The King approached.

"You can pet his face," the King said. "I'll hold you, don't worry."

Lena freed one arm from around her father's neck and twisted to the horse.

"My arm is shaking," she said. "I can't stop it."

"Don't worry. Just stroke his face."

"How?"

"Place your hand at the top of his nose, beneath his eyes. Then, you can scratch him or move your hand down and up, down and up."

Still trembling, Lena willed her hand towards the horse. She touched his nose and stroked.

"Hi," she said. "Hi." Lena gazed at the horse's calm face. "Does he like this, Father?"

"Can't you tell he does? He's not pulling away, is he?"

"No. I guess he doesn't mind my jerky arm."

"His ears also would flatten if he didn't like you. And, look, his ears are perky!"

"I like you, too," Lena said.

"Horses can be great friends," the King said.

"I knew it," Lena said. "I just knew it."

She scratched the horse's nose some more. "This hair feels rougher than I expected," she said.

"Feel between his nostrils," the King said.

Lena moved her hand farther down the horse's nose.

"Doesn't that feel like velvet?" asked her father.

"It really does!"

"The hair on his sides is soft as well. Let me show you." The King walked with Lena to the horse's side.

Lena stared at the horse's bulging stomach.

"Go on," said her father. "You can pet him."

Lena rubbed her hand over the horse's coat. It was hard to believe this was finally happening.

I could pet you forever, she thought.

"His body is so soft!" Lena said. She touched his neck and felt his muscles under her hand. "And, it feels so strong."

"Horses are incredibly strong," her father said. "Just think about it—they carry people, haul coaches and wagons, fight in battles."

"Don't you see, Father?" Lena said. "I'm meant to ride a horse. A horse could be my legs!"

"I do see, Lena," her father said. "I understand." He kissed his daughter's forehead. "Be patient. I'll try to help you. It will take some time. In the meantime, you keep working on your exercises. And, not a word of today to your mother."

44

"I promise." Lena hugged her father's neck. "This is the greatest, happiest thing that's ever happened to me! I love you, Father!"

"I love you, Lena."

Lena looked up to the sunroom balcony. She saw Meg and Fran looking down. Fran was smiling, holding Meg against her. Meg smiled, too—but seemed to be wiping tears off her cheek. Tears of joy? Lena wondered. But, somehow, Lena didn't think so. Something about the look on her twin's face didn't look happy—the smile seemed forced. Something else was going on.

Chapter Nine

"I bet you'll fall right to sleep," Fran said, helping Lena settle against the embroidered pillows. "You had quite a day, Lena."

"It was amazing!" Lena said. "I still can't believe that I finally got to be with a horse! And once my body is strong enough, Father's going to let me ride."

"He is?" Meg asked. "How do you know?"

"He said to be patient—that he'd help me. So he will, I know he will."

Meg slithered under the covers and turned to the side.

"Meg," Lena reached her arm to her sister. "What's wrong?"

"Nothing, I'm tired, that's all," Meg said.

"Meg, I can tell," Lena probed. "I saw the look on your face before. Something about my being with horses bothers you."

Meg was silent.

Fran sat next to her. "Meg, what is it?"

Meg flipped around. "You're braver than I am, Lena! I...I...I'm afraid to be near a horse."

Lena stared at her twin.

Life was so unfair. Meg should have been the one born unable to walk. She never asked to try anything new.

"I thought the only reason you hadn't learned to ride is because I couldn't. That you were just being kind—not doing something for my sake," said Lena.

"Well…that's part of it," Meg said. "I've no reason to ride a horse without you."

"But, now we'll have a chance to learn how to ride horses together," Lena said. "Just think of the adventures we'll have."

"I don't want adventures," Meg said. "Not on a horse."

"But, I don't want to be without you," Lena said.

"What if I don't learn to ride?" Meg asked.

How could this be? Lena thought. Meg was the one who was supposed to be able to do all the things that Lena couldn't. In all of Lena's fantasies about horseback riding, Meg was riding with her.

"Meg," Lena said, "please understand. I need to ride a horse. I'm supposed to—I know that now more than ever. But, I can't imagine going anywhere without you. Please—think about this. There's time to change your mind."

"Meg, would you like me to help you?" Fran offered. "I used to ride horses all the time. It's fun. Really."

Meg swallowed.

"Why don't we find some books in the library about horses? That's always a good way to start," Fran suggested.

Deep down, Meg knew that Lena would ride a horse one day. Lena wouldn't stop working until she did. And, deep down, Meg knew that she would feel awful if Lena rode off on a horse, leaving her behind.

"Okay, Fran, okay. You can help me," Meg said.

Lena grabbed Meg's hand and squeezed it. "Now I'll have a chance to help you do something, Meg. For once! Maybe I can help you!"

"You can try," Meg said. "You and Fran can try."

"Now, it's time for you princesses to go to sleep," Fran said.

"No! Not yet!" Lena said. "We're not going to sleep until we read *Palindrome Discourse*, right Meg?"

"I'll snuff out the candles, Fran. Don't worry," Meg said.

"Don't stay up too late trying to figure it out," Fran said. "Good night."

Chapter Ten

Meg opened to the first page and started reading. "'The idea of the palindrome is closely associated with the material and corporeal aspect of verbal signification.'"

"What? Who could understand that? Keep reading!" Lena said. "Maybe it gets better."

"'Allowing for the reversibility of the linear discourse, the palindrome represents the very idea of transformation and metamorphosis.'" Meg paused.

"I don't understand a word of this," she said.

"I guess you better get our copy of Mr. Stuts' *Book of Words*."

Meg tumbled out of bed and fetched the book from the shelf in their bedroom. "What should I look up first?" she asked. Meg looked back to the essay and reread the first two sentences.

"Since it says that 'the palindrome represents the very idea of transformation and metamorphosis'—let's look up those words," Lena said.

"Okay," Meg said. She turned to the "M's" first— "'Metamorphosis,'" she read, "'a marked change in appearance, character, condition or function. A transformation, as by magic or sorcery!'"

"There's that word 'transformation' again—better look that up," Lena said.

Meg turned to the "T's". "'Transformation," she read, "the act of transforming.'"

"So, what's transforming?" Lena asked.

"'Transform," Meg read, "'is to change markedly the form, appearance, nature, function or condition of something.'"

"So, they basically mean the same thing," Lena said. "They mean change."

"Except," Meg said, her eyes wide, "metamorphosis is when change happens by magic or sorcery! That sounds scary!"

"So," Lena said deep in thought, "the very idea of palindrome means change. Palindrome Pond. How could a pond change things?"

"I have no idea," Meg said. "But, I guess with magic and sorcery it could."

"You think Fran has something to do with magic and sorcery? Like—she's a witch or something?" Lena asked.

"Fran's not a witch!" Meg cried. "She couldn't be!"

"But, she's got a map to this pond."

"How could Fran be involved in something magic? I don't understand," Meg said, shaking her head.

"Well, it's not necessarily a bad thing," Lena said. "Maybe it's good magic."

"If Fran can do magic, why wouldn't she have done magic for us? Why wouldn't she have used magic to help you?" Meg said.

Lena thought. "That's a good question, Meg. A very good question."

"Maybe Fran needs to be at the pond for her magic to work!" Meg said.

"Or," Lena said, "maybe the pond gives you magical powers—like if you drink the water from it! And, then, once you have magical powers you can change things!"

50

"Let's keep reading," Meg said.

Meg picked up the essay again. She read on. "'A palindromic reading of the term "palindrome" itself in its German form (palindrom/mordnilap) points to the idea of murder…and an old name for palindrome is versus diabolicus, which indicates the ancient affinity of the palindrome to magic and sorcery!'"

"Oh no, Lena. There's the magic and sorcery again—but, this time, with murder!"

"Well that doesn't make any sense. What could Fran have to do with murder?" said Lena.

"Fran is the kindest, gentlest person who ever lived," Meg said. "There is no way she would be involved with murdering anyone."

"But she was hiding the map, Meg. And, she didn't want to tell us about it."

"Fran is not a murderer. Besides, if she was, wouldn't she have stopped us reading this book?"

"Maybe. Let's read some more. Can I have a turn?" Lena said.

Meg nodded. She gave Lena the book.

Lena scanned the words. "So many of these sentences are impossible to understand," she said. She kept scanning, trying to find something that made sense.

"Here's something. 'Palindrome invites self-reflection.' That doesn't sound murderous—or magical."

"No," Meg said. "I think it just means thinking about your-self."

"So let's think. Like Mr. Stuts would say, 'What clues do we have?'" said Lena.

Meg began. "Mr. Stuts' *Book of Words* says palindrome is something that reads the same forwards or backwards."

"Right," Lena said. "And, we figured out that the 'new era' phrase written on Fran's map was a palindrome."

"Oh!" Meg said. "And, remember, 'era' meant something like a new time—or new event."

"That's right! I'd forgotten! That makes so much sense! This book says palindrome is mostly about change, and the phrase on the map is about change, too."

"This book also says that palindromes make you think about yourself. If you think about yourself, you might decide to make changes, right?" Meg said.

"You're brilliant, Meg!"

"But, Lena—where do magic, murder and sorcery fit in?"

"I don't know. And, what about the pond? Do you think the pond's water gives you magical powers? Or, maybe it kills you!"

Meg concentrated on all the clues. "Oh! Oh!" she said.

"What?"

"If you look into a pond," Meg said, "what do you see?"

"I don't know—frogs?"

"Think, Lena. What do you see? What do you see in the water?"

"You see yourself!"

"Exactly!" Meg said. "You see your reflection! Get it—your reflection! Self-reflection!"

"Brilliant again, Meg! Brilliant! Fran's pond really may be a place where you can see yourself—and somehow change your life. If that's true, then we *have* to go there."

"But, Lena—magic, murder, sorcery? I think we need to talk to Fran."

"No…not yet," Lena said. "She said she wouldn't tell us anything until we were older. We've got to learn more on our own."

"How?" Meg asked.

"We'll go back to Mr. Stuts. He'll help us. I just know he will!"

CHAPTER ELEVEN

"We want to learn more about palindromes!" Lena said as Mr. Stuts hobbled to where the princesses were standing in the library.

"The book I gave you—wasn't it helpful?"

"Yes…oh yes…what we could understand, that is," said Lena. "Mr. Stuts—we think that Palindrome Pond is a place where you see your reflection and then you can change your life somehow. But we want to know more."

Mr. Stuts tugged at his hair, thinking hard.

"But, it might be dangerous, too," said Meg.

"How so?" Mr. Stuts asked.

"The book says something about murder and sorcery. Here, let me show you," said Meg. She showed Mr. Stuts the murder passage in the book he'd given them. The librarian traced the words with his fingers.

"And your *Book of Words* also says that metamorphosis is change by magic or sorcery," Meg said. "So we think that has something to do with the pond, too."

Mr. Stuts mumbled to himself. He looked at the girls—back at the book—stroked his hair—and mumbled again.

The princesses were perplexed.

"What are you saying?" Lena asked.

He looked up.

Lena resisted speaking. It was hard, but she knew she had to let Mr. Stuts think.

"You are learning that palindromes may hold special powers," he said. "Such powers are not welcomed by everyone. Powers can be misused, or misunderstood."

Lena and Meg looked at each other.

"I don't understand," said Meg.

"Perhaps not everyone wants change...seeks change... welcomes change...not everyone can handle change well," he continued.

"What if you're like me?" said Lena. "I want change more than anything!"

Mr. Stuts looked intently at Lena. "You will change then," he said. "But, you must carefully consider your options. You must...be reflective," he said.

Lena shivered. "You know more about palindromes than you've told us, don't you Mr. Stuts?"

Mr. Stuts said nothing.

"Do you know about the pond?" Meg asked.

Still, Mr. Stuts said nothing. He just gazed at them with calm dark eyes.

"Have you ever heard the palindrome that says something about being drawn onward to a new era?" Lena asked.

Mr. Stuts' mouth twitched. Then, he turned and headed once more to the Philosophy tunnel.

"He knows something," Lena said. "He knows more. I wonder why he won't tell us? Maybe he's a murderer, too!"

"Lena, Fran is not a murderer—and neither is Mr. Stuts! Honestly! You're thinking crazy thoughts!"

"He knows more than he's saying, Meg. And so does Fran," said Lena. "Do you think he knows about Fran's map? Do you think he knows if Fran's a witch?"

Meg frowned, wishing she wasn't thinking what she was thinking. "The book did say all that stuff about magic," she said reluctantly. "And if Fran's a witch, couldn't Mr. Stuts be a sorcerer?"

The sudden sound of Mr. Stuts' uneven steps startled the girls.

He was holding something behind his back. Meg and Lena eyed him uneasily.

Then he held the object out to them and they could see it was only a single sheet of paper. "I found this," he said as Meg took the paper.

"What is it?" she asked. She showed it to Lena. "There is a bunch of numbers scribbled here."

Lena read off the page. "'Double digit palindromes—11, 22, 33, 44, etc.; Triple digit palindromes—121, 131, 141, 242, etc.; four digit palindromes—1221, 1331, 1441, 2112, etc.; palindrome math—121 minus 242 equals –121.'" Lena looked up at Mr. Stuts. "So, palindromes can also be numbers!"

"True," Mr. Stuts said.

Then Lena knew.

"Meg, our next birthday—it will be a palindrome birthday, our first palindrome birthday. We'll be eleven!"

Lena looked up at Mr. Stuts. "You're smiling," she said. "Why?"

"Because," Mr. Stuts said, "you are clever girls. Clever indeed."

"But, what does it all mean?" asked Meg.

"I must return to my work, girls. Be well. Trust in the power of the palindrome."

With that, Mr. Stuts turned and hobbled to his tunnels.

"'Trust in the power of the palindrome!'" Lena said. "What's *that* supposed to mean?"

Chapter Twelve

The King and Queen did not return after two weeks as planned. A messenger had arrived with news that a major earthquake had rattled the central region of the Kingdom, and the King and Queen had gone to assess the damage. It was unclear when they would return.

The princesses' quest to uncover the mystery of Palindrome Pond had stalled. Neither Fran nor Mr. Stuts were offering any additional information or clues for the time-being.

Meg watched Fran carefully for any sign that she might be a witch. So far, nothing suggested it.

Lena decided to concentrate on her exercises, determined to be stronger when her father returned. Maybe then he would agree she was ready to try to ride a horse.

One day, the girls were at work in the sunroom.

Meg and Fran knelt on either side of Lena who was sitting on the wooden floor. Lena was now wearing pants instead of a skirt so she could work on stretching her legs apart. Lena knew her legs would have to stretch much wider in order for her to mount a horse.

Meg and Fran each held one of Lena's ankles and helped guide her legs outward. Lena closed her eyes. She concentrated, willing her legs to open like a scissors. "Stop!" Lena called when the stretch hurt. As much as Lena wished her body would cooperate instantly, she knew from experience it would take time.

"Okay, let's go again," Lena said, just as someone knocked on the door.

"Madam," he said looking at Fran, "a gentleman is here who wishes to meet the princesses."

"A gentleman? Wishes to meet the girls?" Fran said. Never before had this happened. Lena and Meg were not allowed visitors.

"He has papers from the King announcing that he is the new chief of the riding stables."

"That's fine," said Fran. "But why would he want to meet Lena and Meg?"

Lena felt blood rush to her cheeks. "A new chief of the riding stables, Meg! Did you hear?"

"He has gifts for the girls, Madam," said the messenger.

"Show him in! Show him in!" Lena shouted.

The servant looked to Fran.

"His papers are legitimate?"

"Indeed. The King's seal is unmistakable."

"Show him in," she said.

"Maybe Father sent him to me!" cried Lena. "Can you move me to my chair?" she asked.

Meg rolled the chair to her sister. As Fran squatted to lift Lena, a deep voice came from the doorway.

"May I be of assistance?" it asked.

Fran turned her head, bracing Lena against her body. She saw a sturdy man dressed in work clothes standing at the door.

"I've been taking care of the princesses all of their lives," she said. "I can manage."

Fran lifted Lena into her chair.

"You're here to take over the riding stables?" Lena blurted.

"I am," he said, bowing. "My name is Marcus."

"Our father sent you here?" Lena asked.

"Indeed. I met him and your mother, the Queen, on their journey. The King requested my service, so I am here." His voice was gentle. His chest was broad. He looked from Lena to Meg, and then to Fran, as if searching for acceptance. The only one who seemed glad to see him was the child in the wheeled chair.

"I am honored to be here—and honored to meet the princesses at last. Which is which?"

"I'm Lena!"

"I'm Meg." She curtsied, then studied Marcus. Why had Father sent him here? Did this mean they'd be going to the stables soon? She hoped not.

Fran regarded Marcus through narrowed eyes. She stood next to Lena.

"I am Fran," she said, biting off each word. "As I said, I have cared for these girls since their birth. They rarely are without me."

"I can see that they are fortunate, indeed, to have such a loving and capable caretaker," Marcus said bowing once again.

"You brought us gifts?" Lena asked, pointing to packages Marcus held in his hands.

"Yes, indeed, I almost forgot!" He handed one to each girl.

Lena tore at the brown wrapping. Meg undid hers slowly.

"A horseshoe!" Lena exclaimed. She examined it all around.

Meg's package contained the same. Her stomach churned.

"They're for good luck," Marcus explained. "Back home, I was a blacksmith by trade. These horseshoes are from my family's shop. I hope they will bring you good luck."

That made Meg feel better. If this horseshoe brought luck, she wouldn't have to go near a horse anytime soon.

Lena brought her horseshoe to her lips. "Luck!" she celebrated. "They already worked! They brought you to us!"

Chapter Thirteen

For the two weeks following Marcus' arrival, Lena begged Fran every day to take her to the stables to see him. Fran refused. Lena wondered why Marcus hadn't visited her again. Hadn't Father sent him to help her? Could she have been wrong about that? Had the horseshoe's luck already run out?

Lena continued her exercises with a vengeance. Six days a week, she exercised both morning and afternoon. On the seventh, she rested. Meg assisted Lena during one of her daily sessions, and painted during the other. In between, Fran taught the girls their lessons. Once a week they had free time in the library. Lena kept hoping Mr. Stuts would offer them more to read on palindromes; but, no luck there either.

One afternoon, Meg was holding Lena's legs while her sister struggled to sit up, when a tap at the door startled them.

"Marcus!" A smile lit up Lena's face.

Fran helped Lena to sit, then rushed to the door, arms folded tightly across her chest. She stood in front of Marcus, blocking his view of the girls.

"What, may I ask, is the reason for this visit?" she said. "You arrive here unannounced!"

"I was hoping to speak to you in private."

Lena wished that he had come to see her. Then again, she thought, maybe he's here to talk Fran into taking me to the stables. "Go, talk with him!" Lena urged.

Meg's stomach knotted. He was going to suggest they come to the stables, she just knew it. So much for luck.

"I'll just be a moment," Fran said, then stepped into the hallway and closed the door behind her.

"Meg—sneak over there! Try to overhear. Quick!"

Meg scurried to the door and pressed her ear against the heavy wood.

"I can hardly hear a thing," she whispered. "They are far down the hall and they are speaking so softly!"

"Shh—listen and try to hear something, anything!"

Meg tried, but she could only hear the murmur of voices. She could not make out a single word.

Meg backed away from the door just as Fran and Marcus returned.

"Girls, I've asked Marcus to tell you what he just told me." Fran kneaded her hands.

Marcus stood before the princesses. "I have a sister at home. Her name is Clara and she is 20 years old, 13 years younger than I. Like you, Lena, she has problems moving her body."

Lena's eyes widened. It had never occurred to her that anyone else actually was like her. "How so?"

"Her left side has always been stiff and hard to move. She learned to walk, but awkwardly. Her left arm jerks and her left leg won't always move forward in a straight path. Also, it can be hard to understand what Clara says—it seems her tongue won't move the way she wants either."

"She can walk though?" Lena asked.

"She can, but not like Meg, Fran and I can. Her movements are jumpy. She hates leaving the house on her own two feet because lots of people stare at her. When she was young, the kids teased her terribly. They called her names, like 'cripple', and imitated her walk. At one point, she refused to leave the house altogether."

"It's what you said, Fran. People do tease," Lena said.

"They do," Marcus said. "And they can be so terribly cruel."

"That's just not fair," Lena said.

"No one would make the effort to get to know her," Marcus said. "It's like they were scared of her somehow."

"I wouldn't be scared of her," Meg said. "I would get to know her!"

"I'm sure that's true," Fran said.

"Poor Clara," Lena said. "Did she ever leave the house again?"

"Yes," Marcus smiled.

"What happened?" Lena asked.

"When she was about seven she asked me to take her for a ride on a horse. As I told you, we are a family of blacksmiths, so we grew up around horses. Clara spent her days in my father's shop and the horses loved her company. They weren't afraid of her like people were," Marcus said.

"What did your parents say when she asked to ride?" Lena asked.

"They thought it was a wonderful idea. They wanted Clara to get out more. And, I think they knew that people who saw Clara on a horse wouldn't be able to tell she was different."

"So, you took her on a horse?" Meg asked. "Weren't you scared that she might get hurt?"

"I was at first, but I felt I would try anything to bring Clara some happiness."

"That sounds just like how you treat me, Meg."

Meg smiled.

"So, how did you do it? Did Clara learn to ride?" Lena asked almost breathless.

"She did." Marcus said. "I rode on the same horse with her. She leaned against me."

"Did she like it?" asked Lena.

"Oh, yes." Marcus smiled. "I'll never forget our first ride. I had never heard her giggle like that. I rode slowly, of course. Clara didn't care how fast or far we went."

Lena's eyes were dreamy. "Does she ride by herself, now?"

"No, she still rides with me or someone else. She's never asked to learn to ride alone."

"Do you think she could, though?"

"I couldn't say."

Maybe I could ride with someone else on the horse with me, Meg thought.

"Marcus," Lena asked, "did my father see you and Clara riding together?"

Marcus hesitated.

"He did," Marcus said.

"I knew it! Father did send you here for me!"

Marcus didn't respond.

"Do you think I could ride on a horse with you?"

"Eventually. From what Fran told me, you still have to work on the stretch in your legs."

"I will! I will! And, then, can I try?" Lena looked to Marcus. He looked to Fran.

Fran looked at Lena's pleading eyes.

"We'll see," Fran said. "We'll see."

Meg turned away and looked out the window.

"Meg, are you all right?" Fran asked.

"I guess," said Meg. But she sniffled.

Fran put her arms around Meg. "You don't have to go to the stables, you know."

"Is there a problem?" Marcus asked.

"Meg, actually, is fearful of horses."

"Have you ever been on a horse?" he asked.

Meg shook her head no.

"Have you ever been *near* a horse?" he asked.

She shook her head no again.

"Then, it's perfectly understandable that you are afraid. The first thing to do is to meet a horse, and I know just the one. He's very special. Why don't we take a walk to the stables?"

Meg looked at Marcus, then at Lena, than at Fran. She felt she could trust Marcus. It seemed he would look out for her. And Lena wanted this so much. So, hesitantly, she nodded her head.

"I'll do everything I can to help you, Meg. Anything at all," said Marcus. "Horses are my best friends. I think you'll be surprised how much you might like them."

Chapter Fourteen

No one had anticipated that the journey to the stables would be difficult. After all, there was a path that led directly from the castle to the stables and the distance was modest.

But, the path was stony and dotted with ruts. At first, Marcus walked at Lena's side with his arm outstretched across her body to keep her from being jolted out of the chair. Meg, herself, stumbled constantly. And, her long skirt was gathering dust rapidly.

"I see that I have to have this path cleared," Marcus said. He bent over Lena, draped her arms around his neck and scooped her from her chair.

"I can carry her," Fran said. "You take the empty chair."

"Nonsense," said Marcus.

Marcus moved forward with Lena in his arms.

Meg saw Fran's scowl. "You don't like him, do you?" she asked.

Fran pursed her lips. "I suppose I'm just not used to others taking care of you."

They walked on. "Are you feeling okay about this?" Fran asked Meg.

Meg shrugged her shoulders.

"We don't have to go," Fran said.

"I know. But, I want to. I do," Meg said.

When they arrived at the riding stables, Marcus told Fran to leave Lena's chair outside. "The rattling noise it makes could disturb the horses," he said.

Lena took in a deep breath. The air in the barn felt warm in her lungs. A welcoming scent tickled her nose.

Meg stood at the barn's threshold and looked all around. She breathed in and began to cough. "What's that smell?" she asked.

"That's nature!" Marcus replied. "Mostly hay, wood shavings and manure!"

"Manure?" Meg asked.

"Yes, that's horse poop—so watch your step! I see some new droppings that haven't been shoveled yet!" Marcus said.

"Yuk!" Meg said, covering her nose with one hand and lifting her skirt off the ground with the other.

"How many horses are here?" Lena asked, peering left and right.

"Twenty. Lots of the horses are out right now."

"Who are we going to meet?" Lena said.

"A special horse named Invincible. He came here to the castle with me. He was one of Clara's first horses. He's just a couple of stalls down."

Marcus started walking with Lena still in his arms. Meg hesitated, but soon followed behind, skirt in hand, eyes locked on the ground to avoid manure. Fran wrapped an arm around Meg and walked alongside her, trailing Lena and Marcus.

The first stalls were empty. Lena noticed that each had a heavy wooden gate with a window near its top, a floor covered with a deep layer of hay and wood shavings, and buckets hanging from hooks. There were more items hanging outside the

stalls, like blankets, pitchforks, shovels, leather ropes, saddles, and buckets full of brushes.

Marcus stopped in front of a stall where a chocolate-colored horse lay on the hay. His stall gate was open; a metal chain looped across the front to ensure that he would not walk out. The horse looked like a giant dog lying down for a nap. He lifted his head at Marcus' arrival. The horse's mane was black, and a streak of white ran from between his eyes all the way down his nose. He blinked calmly, staring at Marcus and the girl in his arms. Lena noticed a halter around the horse's head.

"This is Invincible," Marcus said. "He likes to lie down much more than most horses. Most horses stay standing, even to sleep!"

Lena was shaking. I belong here, she thought. This is home.

Suddenly, Invincible jerked to his feet and stood up.

"Did I scare him?" Lena asked.

"Don't worry," Marcus comforted. "I'm sure he was just reacting to Meg and Fran's arrival."

Meg cowered behind Fran. "So I scared him?" she quivered.

"This is just a lot of excitement for him, that's all. Stay calm. He won't charge. I promise."

"Breathe slowly," Fran coached, rubbing Meg's back.

"I can't," Meg replied. "The smell is too awful. Deep breaths make it worse!"

"Can I touch him?" Lena whispered.

"Certainly," Marcus said. "Fran, can you remove that chain so we can go in?"

Fran started toward the stall and Meg grabbed her. "Don't leave me!"

"Meg, just stay here. Everything's fine. I'll be right back."

Meg stood frozen in place. Fran did as requested, then returned to Meg's side.

Marcus entered the stall with Lena in his arms. He managed to grab the halter and guide the horse's head toward Lena. Lena felt her stomach dancing.

"Be careful!" Meg called.

"We're fine here, Meg. Truly." Marcus said.

"Now, Lena, can you lean forward just a bit and gently blow into Invincible's nostrils?"

"Blow into his nostrils?"

"Yes, that will allow him to smell your breath. For a horse, that's like telling him your name. Your smell will become familiar to him."

"Wow!" Lena said. She blew gently in the direction of Invincible's nostrils.

Invincible responded with a snort from his nose.

Lena laughed. Meg clutched her stomach.

"Would you like to finger-nibble his mane?" Marcus asked.

"What's that?"

"You bend your fingers like they were teeth of another horse and you open and close them along the hair that stretches from the top of his head to his shoulders."

"Okay, sure! How do I move my fingers?" Lena asked.

"Like this," Marcus said, as he bent Lena's fingers into place and moved them open and closed.

Lena tried to move her fingers like Marcus had. "This is hard!" she said.

"It doesn't have to be exactly like I did. Anything you do will feel good to Invincible."

Lena looked up to Marcus. "Are you sure? I want him to like me!"

"I'm sure," Marcus said.

Lena curved her fingers in and out as best she could and moved them along Invincible's mane.

All at once, Invincible swung his head around and started to nibble at Lena's hands.

"Watch out!" Meg exclaimed.

"Don't worry," Marcus said. "That's his way of returning affection. Now you can tell that he likes you!"

Lena smiled and giggled.

Fran looked at Meg. Still clutching her stomach, Meg's eyes were filling with tears.

"Are you okay?" Fran asked. Lena turned to look at her sister.

"Oh no, Meg, you're crying! Are you scared? Do you need to leave?" Lena asked.

"No. I'm okay. It's just that…well, I see what you mean. You were meant to be with horses," Meg said.

"Thank you, Meg. Thank you," Lena smiled at her twin. She looked up at Marcus. "Are you sure I can't ride with you—right now?"

"I'm sure. Not just yet, Lena. You do need more stretch in your legs. We'll have you back soon enough."

Sooner than you think, Lena said to herself. I'll ride Invincible sooner than you think.

Chapter Fifteen

Lena, Meg and Fran had visited Invincible a few times during the month since their first meeting. Meg still hadn't touched a horse, but she felt more relaxed going to the stables and continued to read horse stories that helped her realize what smart and friendly creatures horses were.

Fran's birthday had arrived, so Lena had a break from exercise while Fran took the day off. The girls were in the library, in search of new books.

"Where did Fran go for her birthday?" Mr. Stuts asked.

"We don't know," Meg said. "She just said she'd be back at the end of the day."

Mr. Stuts hobbled past the girls.

"How old is Fran?" Mr. Stuts asked. "Do you know?"

"She's 33," Lena said.

"Really?" Mr. Stuts replied. "Really?" He stroked his hair.

Lena wondered why the librarian was so interested in Fran. "That's very interesting. Very interesting, indeed," he said.

"Oh!" she gasped. "It's a palindrome birthday for Fran!"

Meg's eyes widened. "33! You're right!"

"So it is!" Mr. Stuts said. "I wonder where Fran went on her palindrome birthday?"

"Do you think that she's at Palindrome Pond?" Meg asked.

"Perhaps," said Mr. Stuts.

"Oh no!" Meg said. "What about the murder? And the sorcery? What if something terrible happens to her there? What if she turns into a witch today?"

Mr. Stuts smiled and shook his head. "Perhaps this will help explain," he said. From his jacket pocket, he pulled out a small worn book. As he extended his arm toward Lena, the hand holding the book began to tremble. Then, his whole arm began to shake. The trembling traveled to his shoulder. Then, his head began to bob down and up uncontrollably.

"Mr. Stuts!" Meg called.

"Are you okay?" Lena asked.

Mr. Stuts spoke in rhythm with his bobbing head, "I'll be fine in just a minute."

And, he was.

The girls stared at the now motionless man.

"You're okay now?" Meg asked.

"Yes, I'm sorry—I'm sorry you saw that. I'm sure it frightened you. Don't worry, I'm fine. Just fine."

"So, this has happened before?" Lena asked.

"Indeed—just a reaction I have now and then," Mr. Stuts said. "Now, how about looking at this." He handed Lena the book.

"*The Diary of Brendan Stovall*," she read. "Who's that?"

"Take a look—see what you can learn." Mr. Stuts lumbered away.

"Do you really think he's all right?" Meg asked as the librarian turned a corner.

"If he says so," Lena said. "And, look, Meg—he's given us another clue!"

"I'm scared, Lena. What if something terrible happens to Fran today?"

"I can't believe that Fran would do anything dangerous. Mr. Stuts certainly doesn't seem worried, does he?"

"True, he doesn't," Meg said. She looked at the book Lena held. "What's this diary?" she asked.

Lena handed it to Meg.

"This looks ancient," Meg said, flipping over the cover. "It feels like the pages might crumble away."

"Be careful, then," Lena said.

Meg gingerly turned to the first page. "Lena! Listen! The first entry is called, "'My Visit to Palindrome Pond!'"

"This is more than a clue!" whooped Lena. "This is the answer! Read it now!"

Meg began:

> I went with great curiosity to the place known as Palindrome Pond. I had been sent there by a philosopher named Robert Stuts who had stayed with me for several months.

"Robert Stuts!" Lena said. "Do you think he's a relative of our very own Mr. Stuts?"

"Maybe! Let's keep reading!" Meg continued.

> Mr. Stuts was a wandering scholar. He traveled from point to point, studying with different people, inviting discussions on the meaning of life. I much enjoyed his company and his teachings. I must confess, he had me quite thoughtful about my place in the world—what my own "life purpose" was, as he called it. We had many fine discussions. The day of his departure, he extended me an invitation to join the Palindrome Pond Society.

"There's a Society? A Palindrome Pond Society?" Lena asked.

> He went on to explain that only a select group of people ever would know about Palindrome Pond and its powers. That only those who were able to reflect on their lives and who wanted earnestly to find their "life purpose" should be allowed to visit the Pond. He had chosen me as one of those few, based on his months of visiting with me.

"Did you hear that, Lena? He was chosen as 'one of those few'?!"

"Oh! 'We few—we few drawn onward!'" Lena clapped. "This is it! Keep reading!"

> He thought I was at a perfect time in my life to experience the pond. He gave me a map. He melted a smudge of purple wax in the bottom right corner and embossed a seal of two interconnecting Ps at the bottom. He told me that I always would know a fellow Pond Society member if I saw this symbol on his person or on his papers.

"That's the same seal that's on Fran's map! That's what that symbol is! It's interconnecting P's" Lena said.

> I followed his instructions and ventured to the pond on my 44th birthday. As I neared the location, I noticed words and numbers carved into tree trunks along the path. 'I saw I was I.' 'I did, did I.' 'I prefer pi.' '12321.' '224422.' I realized that each of these was a palindrome, as it read the same way forward and backward. I came upon a clearing and before me was a perfectly still body of water surrounded by silvery white sand. Sunbeams flooded the area.

I was to recite the palindrome written on the map. Then, to watch the pond. I said the phrase, "Are we not drawn onward, we few, drawn onward to new era?" I waited.

Meg turned the page. She stopped reading.

"Go on!" Lena said.

"The ink's all smudged!" Meg said. "Look!" She showed Lena the book.

"Oh no!" Lena said. "It looks like water spilled on it! We can't read any of this! What happened when he said the phrase? What happened at the pond?"

Meg turned the page again. "Here," she said. "There are a couple more lines I can read."

I reflected long and hard on what I had seen. I realized that I had an opportunity. That the pond has shown me the possibility of building a place to house books. Books that have meant so much to me in my life. A place where books could be shared, one villager to another. I saw that I could help build this place. And, so I did. I did, did I?

"He built a library!" Lena said. "But, we still don't know what happened at the pond!"

Meg shook her head. "Well, when Fran gets back—*if* she gets back—maybe we finally can convince her to tell us more!"

Chapter Sixteen

"Girls! I'm so happy to see you!" Fran rushed into the library and kissed Lena and then Meg on their foreheads. She brushed wisps of hair off her face and caught her breath.

"What's wrong?" Meg asked.

Fran breathed in deeply. "Nothing," she said. She smoothed her skirt. "I'm fine."

"You don't seem fine," Lena said. "You're breathing so hard—did you run here?"

"Well, just from the gate...I just couldn't wait to see you, that's all."

"Something bad happened at the pond, didn't it?" Meg asked, wringing her hands together.

"The pond?" Fran said.

"We know you must have been at the pond," Lena said. "We just read Brendan Stovall's diary—what wasn't smudged."

"Really?" Fran let out a long breath. "I see...perhaps...perhaps I should chat with Mr. Stuts...and then, we'll talk. Do you know where he is?"

"Back in the History Tunnel," Lena said.

"Thanks. You're both okay? You'll wait here for me?"

The girls nodded. Fran lifted her hem and scurried away.

"Something bad happened at the pond," Meg said. "Something spooked her! See? Murder! Sorcery! There is something scary about that place!"

"Let's go to the tunnel entrance—there's a good echo there—maybe we can hear something."

Meg moved Lena to the tunnel entrance. In her hurry, Fran had left the door wide open.

Fran's voice traveled toward them. "I'm telling you! She looked dead!"

They heard Mr. Stuts next. "We'll have to be mindful, then. It doesn't have to come to pass. Choices can be made."

"But, the pond. They know about it now. You showed them Stovall's diary?"

"True. I got carried away. I've never done that before. I told them too soon." Mr. Stuts voice paused. "Well, they gave you your map back. Correct?"

"Correct. And I don't suppose they could know how close the pond is to this castle." Fran paused and pictured the map in her mind. "I'm sure I didn't label my drawing of the castle in any way that would identify it as our own."

"Good. The pond's location will remain a mystery…for now. Share with them what you wish about your own trips there."

"So, Mr. Stuts does know about the pond!" Lena whispered. "He *must* be related to the Stuts in Stovall's diary! And Fran is the one who drew in the castle on the map!"

The girls heard footsteps. Meg pulled Lena's chair swiftly back to their original spot.

"Did you hear that? Someone looked dead! And, now they're worried that we know about the pond!" Meg whispered.

Fran returned. She sat down at a table next to Lena's chair.

"Have a seat, Meg," she said. "It's time we talked about Palindrome Pond."

Chapter Seventeen

"Palindrome Pond is a magical place," Fran began.

"What's the magic?" Lena asked. "That's the part that was smudged in Stovall's diary."

"The magic," Fran continued, "is…if you go to the pond on a palindrome birthday—and you stare at your reflection on the water's surface—and you say the magical palindrome…"

"You mean the one about 'drawn onward to new era?'" Meg asked.

"Yes, that's right," Fran said.

"Then?" Lena asked, twisting her hands in knots.

"Then, the calm still surface of the water begins to shift. The water moves in tiny waves in one direction, as if a wind is blowing on it, and your reflection disappears and other images appear on the surface of the water."

"Like paintings?" Meg asked.

"Yes, much like paintings are appearing."

"All at once?" Meg asked.

"No. One after another. The first images are all from the past. Then, the water begins to move, in the other direction. It's as if once you've taken stock of your past, you're ready to glimpse your possible future. And, so, you see pictures of things you've never seen before."

"The future!" Lena's hands clasped in front of her mouth.

"That's right," Fran said. "The future."

"Meg, can you believe it? A place where we could see how life will change!"

"How life *could* change, Lena. The future isn't definite—not even the future that the pond reveals. You still can make choices to change the future," Fran said.

That's what Mr. Stuts must have meant. "Choices can be made," Meg recalled him saying. So, maybe the dead person Fran saw doesn't have to die. Maybe that future can change. She wondered what Fran would tell them.

"What have you seen there?" Meg asked.

"I first visited the pond when I was twenty-two."

"How did you find out about it?"

"I lived with many other families before I came here. The mother of the last family with whom I stayed, she is the one who gave me the map. The one who made me a member of the Palindrome Pond Society. She told me it was clear I was still looking for my true place, my true purpose in life. She thought perhaps the pond could help me find it. And, it did."

"What do you mean?"

"The pond is where I first saw pictures of the two of you."

"You saw us? Lena and me? In the pond?"

"I did, indeed. I saw this castle, and your parents, and your mother pregnant. And then I saw two babies. And I saw your mother and father holding one another, with worried looks on their faces. I saw them trying to get you to sit up as a baby, Lena. I saw them crying. I saw that I was needed, at this castle. So, I searched for it. I searched for you."

"You came looking for us?" Meg's arm naturally reached to her twin. "You came here just to be with us?"

"I did. I was drawn here. I chose to seek you out. I wandered through the forest. Eventually, I met someone and asked where the castle of this kingdom was. He pointed me here. As soon as I saw this place, I recognized it from the pond. I knew I had found where I belonged."

"Drawn onward!" Lena said. "Just like the palindrome phrase says!"

"But," Meg said, "I thought we weren't born yet when you arrived? You've told us you were here before we were."

"It's true. Your mother didn't realize she was pregnant yet. When I arrived here, I spoke to your parents about my life and told them I had a vision that I was meant to be here. To help them. I didn't tell them about the pond—you know now that you must be chosen, selected specially, to learn about the pond. So, I just said that I had a vision and that in my vision they had two babies, and that they would need help with them. Your parents had been hoping for a baby. They decided to take me in. As you know, your mother gave birth to you the following year."

"You came to us through magic!" Lena said. "See, Meg, that's good magic—not bad."

Meg still felt uneasy in her stomach. "So...you're not a witch?"

Fran chuckled. "No! My goodness! No! Is that what you thought?"

Meg nodded. "What did you see today?"

"Today, I saw my family."

"You're leaving us, aren't you? You're going home to your real family!" Meg said.

"No, no, Meg. I didn't see my family in the future...I saw them in my past."

"The first part of the pond's magic!" Lena said.

"Yes, that's right," Fran said.

"And, I think I know why the pond showed them to me... why I needed to remember that part of my past just now..."

Chapter Eighteen

"When I was little, I lived on a farm with my mother and father. I had no brothers or sisters. I worked the farm with my parents from sunrise to sunset. At night, after dinner, my father would sit in his rocking chair and read. He read to himself and he read to me. My mother, she didn't know how to read. No females in my kingdom did. It was considered unladylike."

"Reading, unladylike?" Lena said.

"I know for you that is hard to believe. But, it's true. Still, I knew I wanted to read. Just like you, Lena, feel you are meant to ride a horse…I felt I was meant to read. I begged my father to teach me. Finally, he did."

"And, the pond reminded you of that today?" Meg asked.

Fran's eyes teared. "Yes."

"What did you see?"

"I saw myself sitting next to my father. He was leaning next to me and showing me a book."

"What happened to your father?" Meg asked.

Fran wiped a tear off her cheek. "I don't know what happened to him. I ran away."

"Why?"

"Because, I had learned how to read."

"I don't understand," Lena said.

"My father gave me the gift of reading. But, when it came time for me to marry, when I was eighteen, it became clear that my ability to read was an incredible problem."

"What happened?" asked Lena.

"My parents had arranged for my marriage to a merchant in the town. They were so pleased because I wouldn't have to spend my life doing hard farm work like they did."

"What do you mean—they arranged for your marriage?" asked Meg.

"In my kingdom, ladies do not choose their husbands. Parents choose husbands for their daughters."

"That sounds like an awful place. You can't read and you can't choose your husband!" Lena said.

"Certainly different from what you know," Fran said. "At first, I *was* willing to marry the man they had chosen for me. He seemed kind and he was known as a generous man to people who had less than he. But, in the end, I couldn't marry him."

"Why not?"

"He came to visit at our farm several weeks before the wedding. When he arrived, I was reading in my father's rocking chair. He saw me and asked if I was actually reading or just looking at the book. I met his eyes directly. 'Actually reading,' I replied. He stared at me, then motioned for my father to speak with him outside."

"I overheard bits and pieces of the conversation.'Who taught her to read?…not fit to be a wife…no one will have her…she has to stop.' When he finished talking, I saw my father shake his hand. I couldn't believe what I was seeing. How could my father agree to such demands? So, I bolted."

"You just left?" Meg asked. She couldn't imagine running off alone.

"I did."

Meg went to Fran and hugged her.

"Do you wish your father hadn't taught you how to read?" Lena asked.

"Goodness no," Fran said. "Reading means so much to me. I can't imagine life without Homer, Aristotle, Aristophanes. Their stories and writings help shape my own thinking—about life and dreams and struggles. No...no regrets. Reading is like water to me."

"Like riding a horse will become water for me," Lena said.

Fran looked at Lena. "Perhaps." Then, Fran grinned. "And, you know, if I didn't know how to read, I would never have been your nanny. So, in part, I think I was meant to read because I was meant to be with you!"

Meg hugged Fran close to her.

"What about your mother?" Lena asked. "How did your mother feel about your reading?"

"Mixed," Fran said. "She was scared that it would cause me problems—which, of course, it did. But, she was happy for me because I loved it and I think she knew it would bring me opportunities she never had."

Fran paused. Her eyes glazed over.

"What is it?" Meg asked.

Fran's voice cracked. "I try not to think about how she must have felt when I left."

The princesses were silent.

Then, Lena thought back to how they had started this conversation.

"Wait! Fran," Lena said. "We still don't know what the pond showed you about your future!"

Chapter Nineteen

"The future!" Lena said. "Tell us! What's in your future?"
Fran hesitated.

"It's bad, isn't it?" Meg asked. "That's why you seemed so frazzled when you came in today?"

"No—no, it's okay. And...something I need to make clear again. The pond shows you a possible future," Fran said. "You still have choices to pursue that future."

"Like, when you were twenty-two and you chose to come looking for us?" Meg asked.

"That's right, Meg. Exactly. I didn't have to look for this castle. I chose to. I felt I was meant to."

"So what did you see this time, Fran? Tell us!" said Meg.

"Tell us! Please!" Lena was so excited she nearly tumbled out of her chair.

"Something I want to avoid." Fran hesitated.

Finally, she said, "I saw Marcus."

"Marcus? You want to avoid Marcus?" Lena said. "Why? He's wonderful!"

"Calm down, Lena," Fran said. "I didn't say I wanted to avoid Marcus. I saw him—with both of you—and horses."

"Were we riding?" Lena asked.

Fran nodded.

"Both of us?" Meg asked.

"Yes, both of you."

"Was anyone on the horses with us?" Lena asked.

Fran paused. "You were on the horses alone. And, that is what I wish to avoid!"

"I'll be able to ride on my own...I knew it!" Lena said. Then Lena realized what Fran had just said. "What do you mean you want to avoid that? I'm meant to ride, and to ride alone, like you were meant to read!"

"Only if we choose that, Lena," Fran cautioned.

"Well, I choose it!"

"What else did you see?" Meg asked, hoping to distract her sister.

Fran blushed and looked at the ground. "Something else I think I will choose to avoid. And that is all I have to say on that topic."

"But Fran...!" said Lena.

"No, Lena. I think we've talked quite enough about the pond today. In fact, I think it best if you two forget that the pond even exists. Come on, now. It's time for your exercises."

Meg stared in surprise when, instead of arguing, Lena said "You're right."

But, as Fran lifted her from her chair, Lena added to herself, "There is nothing else to talk about. Because I am going to ride by myself someday. I have nine months to practice riding before we turn eleven—our first palindrome birthday. Once I can ride a horse, I'll get to the pond...even if I have to go myself."

Chapter Twenty

After hearing about Fran's visit to the pond, Lena worked even harder at her exercises. And she never mentioned Palindrome Pond again—not to Fran, or Mr. Stuts, or even to Meg.

Fran was relieved.

But Meg was worried. She knew her sister better than anyone. Lena was definitely up to something. Meg tried to talk with Fran about it, but the nanny told her she was being silly. Lena was just concentrating on preparing for her first ride on Invincible, Fran said.

When the day for Lena to ride Invincible finally came, Lena was awake earlier than usual. She wished she could just run to the stables and mount Invincible by herself. But, as always, she had to wait for other people to assist her and ready her. It seemed as if hours passed before Fran arrived to dress her. At long last, the girls and Fran were on their way to the stables.

"Invincible is ready for you!" Marcus said as he welcomed the trio.

"Where's the saddle?" Lena asked.

"We couldn't both fit. Besides, Clara had an easier time keeping her balance if she sat on a blanket instead of a saddle. She could feel the horse's body moving. You have two handles to hold on to—see them? They're on this belt that's wrapped around him."

"Okay. How do I get up there?" Lena asked.

"I taught Invincible to kneel down for Clara. First, he'll kneel, then I'll mount him. Fran, can you lift Lena up here?"

"Of course."

Lena watched as Marcus reached for a handle on the belt and hoisted himself onto the horse. He nodded to Fran.

This was it. It really was. Lena couldn't believe that she was about to ride Invincible. Invincible—who was strong. Who could walk. Who could take her places she wanted to go...places like Palindrome Pond.

Fran lifted Lena, and Marcus grabbed the excited girl under her arms. Fran helped position Lena's legs over Invincible. Lena winced.

"Are your legs feeling okay?" Marcus asked.

"They feel a little stretched, but fine," Lena said.

Marcus guided Lena's hands to the handles on the belt and adjusted her so she was settled comfortably on Invincible's back. Lena wobbled a bit. Fran flung her hands up towards the princess.

"I'm fine! I'm fine!" Lena cried out. There was no way she'd tell anyone how scared she suddenly was.

Meg clasped her hands over her mouth. She couldn't imagine being up there.

"Lean back against Marcus," Fran directed. "Don't lean away from him. Please! Be careful."

"Are you okay? Shall I have him stand?" Marcus asked.

"Yes, yes!"

Marcus tugged on the reins and Invincible stood. Lena's body jerked as the horse repositioned his front legs, but Marcus held her steady.

"Don't fall!" Meg called out. No, she decided, she could never get on a horse.

"I'm fine!" Lena said. She looked around. "Meg, you have to see how the world looks from up here! It's beautiful! Look how tall I am!"

"Shall we take a little walk?" Marcus asked.

"Please! Please!"

"Fran, why don't you walk next to us? We'll just take a walk, close to the stable. Let's see how Lena does," Marcus said. "Lena, can you cluck with your tongue."

"Like this?" Lena moved her tongue against the roof of her mouth until she made a sound like one of the barnyard chickens.

Invincible began to walk. "Yes, like that. Invincible understood!"

Lena laughed. She wanted to crow like the old rooster who ruled the chicken coop. Her body, braced securely by Marcus, swayed with Invincible's steps. Fran walked directly at their side.

"Look at me, everyone!" Lena called. "I'm here! I'm on Invincible! I'm riding a horse."

Lena turned her head, looking all around as Invincible sauntered. She savored the feeling of movement without the cold, stiff sides of her wooden chair pressed against her body. You and I can go places, Invincible, Lena said to herself. Just you and me. I won't need anyone to push me in my chair. I won't have to wait for anyone to decide when to move. *I'll* get to decide. *I'll* get to choose the direction. No one else. Just me. Just me and you.

Lena leaned against Marcus' firm chest. "Thank you, Marcus," she said. "Thank you, Invincible."

Meg watched intently. She had never seen Lena smile so wide or for so long. Scary as it was watching her sister on a horse, and, scary as it was being this close to a horse herself, she could tell Lena was where she was meant to be.

"How's she doing, Marcus?" Fran asked.

"Really well. I'm bracing her, but I can tell she's got more balance and strength in her torso than I had anticipated. I'm not worried about her at all."

"So, does that mean you'll ride with me again?" Lena asked.

"It does," Marcus replied.

"And again, and again, and again!" Lena cried. Then she threw back her head and cheered. Anyone who heard her would have known that joy pulsed through her veins.

Chapter Twenty-One

In the month that followed Lena's first ride, Fran and the twins went to the stables every day. Lena invented ways she could continue her exercises there. She had Fran prop her against a bale of hay in the stables so she could work her legs by pushing her feet against crates filled with tools. She had Fran lay a blanket on the floor outside Invincible's stall so she could work on pulling herself to a sitting up position. Once she started riding, Lena realized that she needed to work on her finger, hand and arm control if she ever wanted to hold Invincible's reins herself. So, Marcus tied ropes to a crate, then had Lena pull the crate toward her to strengthen her arms. He had her braid small ropes together to strengthen her fingers and hands.

As time passed, Lena could push heavier crates with her feet and sit up by herself more easily. Her rope braids got longer and tighter.

Marcus and Lena rode Invincible together daily. If it rained, they rode indoors in a dirt ring covered by a thatch roof. Lena loved the pattering sound of the rain on the thatch, the smell of the sandy ground and the feel of Invincible moving beneath her. In the beginning, Fran walked at Lena's side. But, Marcus soon convinced her that Lena's balance was quite solid.

The first day that Lena and Marcus rode without Fran hovering at the horse's side, Lena felt as if she were a butterfly who had been freed from its cocoon. Without Fran crowding her, she was only one step away from riding alone.

Meg came to the stables daily, wearing pants like Lena's. She painted while Lena rode. Meg had yet to touch Invincible or any other horse, but she soon admitted her fascination with the beautiful creatures. She experimented with different brush strokes to express the horses' gentle strength and fluid motions.

Meg also could see that Lena was becoming more and more comfortable riding. Sooner or later, Meg knew, she was going to have to get on a horse herself. Or Lena would ride away without her.

One day, watching Marcus and Lena round the far side of the stable yard, Meg took a deep breath. Before she could change her mind, she turned to Fran and asked, "Would you be able to ride a horse with me? The way that Marcus and Lena ride together?"

"Of course!" Fran said. "I was hoping you'd ask me one of these days!"

"I'm still really scared."

"I know."

"But, I don't like Lena riding without me."

"I understand. I want you to know, I think you are very brave."

"I'm not brave at all. I'm scared."

"That's what bravery is, Meg. When you are scared, but you go forward anyhow."

Meg liked hearing that she was brave.

"So my courageous princess, which horse do you think we should ride?"

Meg had a favorite, Jackson. He was a grey and white speckled horse she'd painted often. If she was going to ride, he would be the one.

She and Fran walked outside to wait for Marcus and Lena.

"Marcus, Meg has asked if she and I can ride a horse together."

"Hooray!" Lena cried. "Meg, really?"

Meg nodded. Too late to back out now.

"That makes me so so so happy! I've missed you not doing this with me! You'll love it, I promise. You'll want to paint everything you see from so high up!"

"I couldn't be more pleased myself," Marcus said. "Do you want to try right now?"

"I think I better while I've got my nerve up."

"Okay. I'll have the stable hand get Jackson ready for you."

"How did you know I wanted him?"

"Oh, I don't know," grinned Marcus. "Maybe all those paintings of him?"

Meg smiled back, but gulped as a stable hand arrived with Jackson, looking much bigger than he did on her canvases.

"Are you sure he won't throw me off?" she asked.

"Jackson wouldn't do that," Marcus assured her. "He's the gentleman of the stable."

"Next to Invincible, that is," Lena bragged.

"I'll mount him first, Meg," Fran said. "Then I'll brace you when you get up, okay?"

Meg nodded.

Fran hoisted herself onto Jackson, her skirt bunching up above her knees as she straddled him. Casey, the stable hand, lifted Meg onto the horse in front of Fran. Meg grabbed the belt handles so tightly her knuckles turned white—almost as white as her face. She kept her eyes riveted on Jackson's freckled neck.

"Can you try to sit up tall?" Fran asked. "You'll be more comfortable, I promise."

Meg took a deep breath and sat as straight as she could.

"Great! Great job!" Fran said.

Meg's tight face began to relax. She let her eyes wander. She looked down at the ground.

"It would be quite a fall down, wouldn't it?" she asked.

"Meg, you won't fall. But, you know what? Even if you did, you'd be fine. Ready to go?"

Meg gave the slightest of nods. "We won't go fast, and we won't go far. Would you like Casey to walk next to us the way I used to walk next to Lena?" Fran asked.

Meg nodded.

"Okay, let's go," Fran said.

Fran gave Jackson a gentle squeeze with her legs. Meg tensed up with the horse's first step. But the slight rocking motion of Jackson's gait calmed her.

"Why, it's really like being in a moving rocking chair," she thought. Then Meg spied Lena, whose grin was almost as wide as it was the day of her own first ride.

"You're riding, Meg!" she called. "You are! Isn't it great?"

Meg wasn't ready to admit to "great." But, it wasn't bad.

"This is just the beginning, Meg! We're together again! We're a team!"

Chapter Twenty-Two

Fran and Meg joined Marcus and Lena on their daily rides. Meg became increasingly at ease. She even admitted to Fran that she was enjoying herself.

"The only thing I don't like about riding is the time it takes away from my painting," she said.

One balmy sunny day, Marcus offered an idea. "Now that we're all riding horses," he said, "why don't we take a ride on an easy trail?"

"Yes. Oh, please! Yes!" Lena said.

"Will you be fine with that, Meg?" Fran asked.

"I think so. It would be fun to see some sights."

"We won't ride for long. But, it will be a nice change," Marcus said.

"An adventure!" said Lena, thrilled that she finally could explore.

"Fine. I'll get the horses ready."

But, as Marcus was slipping the bit between Invincible's teeth, a page appeared at the stables.

"I have a message from the King and Queen," he said, handing Fran a piece of paper.

"Open it," Meg said. "Maybe they'll be home soon!"

I hope not, Lena thought. As soon as Mother returns, she'll be furious about my riding. Please stay away.

Fran opened the note. "'Our darlings,'" Fran read. "'We miss you terribly. We have seen extreme destruction in many villages and have been gratified to be of some help to our subjects. We have traveled farther and longer than we ever anticipated, as the earthquake impacted more terrain than we had realized. By the time you receive this note we expect to be on our way home. Be safe. We hope to see you within the month.'"

"Another month!" Meg sighed.

Another month! Lena rejoiced to herself.

"I have to try to ride Invincible by myself!" Lena declared. "I can't wait any longer!"

"By yourself?" Fran asked, startled. "Lena, I thought this was settled. It's too dangerous."

"But, Marcus thinks I can," said Lena.

Fran glared at Marcus.

"Fran," Marcus said. "Please don't be upset. I never *promised* Lena that she could ride alone. But, I have told her, and I am telling you, that I do think she is capable of that. When we ride together she doesn't brace herself against me at all. She handles the reins alone. Her balance is secure. Quite frankly, I feel like I'm not needed at all."

"You won't stop me, will you Fran? It's my dream, my life purpose!"

"Your life purpose, Lena, may include riding a horse…but not necessarily alone," Fran said. "What if you lost your balance?"

"You told Meg that she would be all right if she fell off. Why is it different with me?"

"It's different, Lena. You know that."

"I don't see that it is any different," Lena protested. "Please! I need to try to do this alone. Think of all the things I'll always need help with, including getting on a horse. Once I'm on him, let me ride alone. Please. Let me do something by myself!"

Fran looked at Marcus.

"I defer to you on this decision," Marcus said.

"As you should," Fran snapped.

"Please, Fran. Please," Lena begged.

"You must not even think, for one moment, of directing Invincible to trot or even to walk at a pace faster than a snail!"

Lena flung her arms over her head. She pumped them up and down. "Thank you! Oh, thank you!"

"What about me?" Meg spoke up.

"What do you mean?" Fran asked.

"Do you think I'm ready to try to ride alone?"

"That's up to you, Meg. Do you feel ready?"

"Well, I'm not leaning against you any more either. Right?"

"Absolutely correct."

"And, I've learned to use the reins and my legs to direct Jackson."

"True."

"So, maybe I'll try."

"Meg," Lena said. "You are the best twin sister anyone could ever have!"

Chapter Twenty-Three

"I'm in heaven!" Lena announced. She was on Invincible, all by herself. Fran stood next to Invincible's side, stroking the white stripe on his nose.

"Lena, I'm happy for you that you're up there," Fran said. "But, I must tell you that we're going back to me walking next to you as you ride. I'm not ready for you to just go off on your own."

"Okay," Lena said.

Lena stroked Invincible's neck. She wanted to direct him to move, to take off and go somewhere—anywhere.

Soon, I'll go where I want—like to Palindrome Pond, she thought. I'll get there. I know I will. My life is finally going to be what I want. But, not yet. Not now.

Meg was standing near her, preparing to mount Jackson all alone for the first time. Lena knew that Meg wanted her close by—and Lena wanted to be there.

"Are you ready to mount Jackson?" Marcus asked Meg.

Meg felt a tight knot in her stomach. She had grown accustomed to riding with Fran. She felt scared all over again.

Meg looked at Lena.

I wish I could be like her, Meg thought. She's the one who should be scared and she isn't at all.

Lena noticed her sister's hesitation. "Meg—you don't have to ride alone, you know. Don't do it for my sake. You still can ride with Fran. It's okay."

"I want to be able to do what you do, Lena. I'm getting on by myself. I am."

"Take deep breaths, Meg," Fran counseled. "Think how far you've come already. Truly, you know how to do this. You've been handling Jackson on your own without even realizing it. I've just been along for the ride."

Meg looked at Jackson. "Marcus, there's a saddle on him. I've never ridden with a saddle before."

"It's easy," Marcus said. "You take these reins in your left hand. Then, you put your left foot in this stirrup, stretch your right hand to grab the back of the saddle, and hoist yourself up. Then, your right foot goes in the other stirrup. Once you're up, you can grab the horn to secure yourself."

Meg swallowed hard.

"Marcus, will you spot me?"

"My pleasure," he said.

Marcus stood next to Jackson. "Come here, Meg, come closer. Here are the reins. Now, left foot in this stirrup. Good. Now, reach your hand to the back of the saddle. That's right. Now, swing your right leg over Jackson's back. Great. Now, is your right foot in the other stirrup?"

Meg's right foot dangled. She swept it back and forth in search of the stirrup. Her heart started racing. Where was the stirrup? She couldn't find it. She leaned to the right and lost her balance.

She rolled over the right side of Jackson and fell onto the dirt.

Lena's heart skipped a beat as she heard a loud thump.

"Meg!" Lena cried. "Are you all right? Oh no, oh no!"

"Meg!" Fran called, straining her neck to see her.

Marcus rushed to Meg who was splayed on the ground. He helped her to sit.

"Are you all right?" he asked.

She brushed off dirt from her clothes. She took a deep breath.

"My side feels sore, but I don't think it's really hurt."

"Thank goodness," Fran mumbled.

"Meg, please just ride with Fran. It's okay!" Lena said.

"No. No. I'm not going to do that. I'm glad I fell off. Now I know what it feels like. It's not so bad, really."

"I'm not sure about this at all," Fran said. "I think we should stop. It's enough that we all ride together."

"No, I'm going to try again." Meg walked around Jackson and put her foot in the stirrup.

"Wait," Fran said.

"Fran," Lena protested. "You've got to let us do this."

"Didn't you see what just happened to Meg? I am responsible for your safety. What if you had been the one to fall?"

"So? Meg didn't get hurt. I wouldn't either. It's not as if we ever let the horses walk fast. We'll never take a terrible fall."

"Fran," Meg said. "I really do want to do this."

Fran sighed. "All right. But, this is going to be a very short ride. Just here, around the stables. And Marcus and I will be walking next to you."

"Yes!" Lena said. "Go on, Meg!"

Meg took in a deep breath. She concentrated. She looked at Lena one more time. I'm getting up there where she is, Meg said to herself.

"Don't think about it too much," Marcus advised. "Just feel it, with your body. You'll be fine."

Meg let out her breath. She planted her left foot in the stirrup. Just feel it, she thought. Just reach for the back of the saddle, pull up, straddle Jackson and find the other stirrup. There! There!

Meg pushed her heels into the stirrups and noticed how sturdy they felt. She sat tall on Jackson's back.

"You're okay?" Lena asked.

"I am! I made it!"

Lena grinned at her twin. Compelled as she had been to learn to ride a horse without Meg, she was so much happier that Meg was now joining her.

"A short ride, ladies," Fran said. "Just right around here."

"Ready, sister?" Lena asked.

Meg took a deep breath. "Ready."

"Let's ride!" Lena shouted.

"Slowly," cautioned Fran.

With a simultaneous clucking of their tongues, the girls directed their horses to move forward. Invincible and Jackson ambled side by side.

Even though Fran once again was hovering next to Lena as she rode, Lena felt free. She was in charge. She alone held the reins. She was a butterfly free of her cocoon—ready to fly. This was how she would get to Palindrome Pond, and to the village, and everywhere else. Just like she had dreamed. With Meg by her side.

Lena looked at her sister.

"I love you, Meg!" Lena called out. "I love you—and Invincible, and Marcus and Fran!" Lena laughed and laughed.

Meg turned to her sister. "I never thought I could do this. I can't believe how easy it feels!"

"Bravery runs in this family, I see," Marcus said, keeping pace next to Jackson. "You ladies remind me of old Invincible here."

"What do you mean?" Lena said.

"Do you know what 'invincible' means?" he asked.

"It means 'strong' doesn't it?" Meg asked.

"Not just strong," Marcus replied. "No, not just strong. It means unconquerable. Incapable of being defeated."

Lena smiled. "You think we are unconquerable?"

"I most certainly do. Just look at the two of you. Lena, your body may not function the way you want it to. But, your spirit, your drive, it's incapable of being defeated. You never give up. You're up there, because of your invincible spirit."

"What about me?" Meg asked. "How am I invincible?"

"You, Meg. Three months ago you didn't want to go near a horse. You didn't want to come to the stables. Now, here you are. On a horse. Riding one yourself. If that's not invincible, I don't know what is."

"So, how *did* Invincible get his name?" asked Lena, stroking her horse's shoulder.

"Let's have a snack, and I'll tell you the story of your brave horse, Lena. I think he was meant to be yours all along."

Chapter Twenty-four

"When Invincible was born, his name was Stripe."

"Because of his nose?" Meg asked.

"That's right," Marcus replied.

The girls were sitting on a blanket in the indoor riding ring.

"When Stripe was just about a year old, he was grazing in the open field with the other horses. My father, brothers and I were working in the blacksmith shop. We heard the horses start to neigh. My father looked out the window and saw a storm approaching. A band of dark, greenish gray clouds was racing toward us. Lightning flashed in the sky, followed by rumbles of thunder.

"We dropped our tools and ran to get the horses to safety. At first, I didn't see Stripe. Then, I spied him at the far end of our property, against the fence. He was neighing frantically. I could see that something was wrong. Each time the thunder clapped, Stripe stomped his left leg, but he couldn't seem to break free. I ran to him. His right foot was caught in the wooden fence. I ran back to the shop to get an axe. By the time I cut Stripe free, he had an enormous gash in his leg."

"He was bleeding?" Lena asked.

"Oh, yes. I could see right to his bone, the cut was so deep."

"What happened next?" Meg asked.

"I used the lead to tie his injured foreleg to the other part of his leg—folded back, like this." Marcus demonstrated by bending his left calf against his left thigh.

"Why do that?" Lena asked.

"So he wouldn't put any weight on it," Marcus said. "By then, it was raining so hard I knew no one would hear my voice if I yelled for help. So, we started to the stables. Stripe would take several hopping steps, rest, and then hop some more. We were drenched by the time we got to the stables, but, we made it. I settled Stripe in his stall and went to the house to get warm water to clean his wound. Lightning must have hit the stables, because, when I went back outside, the building was ablaze. Flames were shooting in every direction."

"Why didn't the rain put out the fire?" Meg asked.

"The fire quickly spread to the inside of the stable," Marcus said. "The rain was of no help then. We ran around the building, searching for a safe route in. We couldn't find one. We had eight horses in there—and only one survived."

"Invincible," Lena whispered.

"That's right. We stood there watching, helpless as the walls starting collapsing. And then, hobbling through the black smoke and flames, we saw Stripe."

Marcus patted the horse's side. "Brave, fierce, determined. He escaped the fire, but still had to survive his burns and the wounded leg. We weren't sure he was going to make it."

"Why not?" Lena asked.

"Because the burns and the cut could have become infected. The doctor worried he might lose his leg. And that would mean we would have to put him down. A horse really can't live without one of its legs. They need to stand much of the time to stay healthy."

"So, if I had been a horse, I'd have been killed?" Lena asked.

"Horses are different, Lena," Marcus said.

"Did you almost kill Invincible?"

"We agreed we couldn't make that decision until Stripe had a chance to heal. The doctor stitched up his wound and instructed us to soak it in salt water four times a day, to change his bandage dressing four times a day, and to clean his stall any time there was any manure to try to keep out germs that could cause infection. He also taught us how to care for the burns with ointments. The doctor warned us that even if the wound healed enough for Stripe to walk, he might never be rideable."

"Was Invincible in a lot of pain?" Lena asked.

"If he was, we never knew it. He was friendly. He ate well. He lay down a lot. I think that's why he still likes to. And, every day he tried to stand. Every single day. Many times a day."

"After two weeks, he finally managed to haul himself up. But, he really couldn't put any weight on the injured leg. So, he stood still for a bit, then lay back down. Every day he repeated this—and, soon enough, he was able to stand on his injured leg for minutes, then hours. One day he hobbled out of his stall."

"This horse does sound like the equine version of Lena, doesn't he?" Fran asked.

"Yes. I've been reminded of Invincible's recovery every time I've seen Lena doing her exercises over and again without complaint," Marcus said.

"When did you decide to rename him?" Meg asked.

"One evening at dinner, we marveled that he had survived the leg wound and the fire. So, my father suggested we rename him. Invincible, the unconquerable!"

"And now he's my horse, right Marcus?" Lena asked.

"He is, indeed," Marcus said. "Invincible and invincible—quite a pair."

Chapter Twenty-five

For several weeks Lena and Meg rode every day, Fran and Marcus walking beside them. They chose to master their solo riding skills close to the stables instead of riding trails with Marcus and Fran on the horses with them. After the princesses had proved they could manage the horses, Lena decided it was time to ask if they could venture further.

"Can we go out on a trail?" she said.

Marcus turned to Fran. "What do you think?"

"Is there somewhere we can go that's close by—where the trail is wide?" she replied.

"We could go to the meadow. It's quite beautiful and an easy ride. We could have a picnic lunch."

"Is there any water there?" Fran asked.

Marcus looked puzzled. "No, no water at all," he said.

Ignoring the question in his voice, Fran nodded and they were soon on their way.

They ambled onto a path surrounded by tall grasses and brightly colored wildflowers. The horses' tails made swishing sounds as they brushed the grass.

"Can you smell the flowers, Meg?" Lena said.

Meg took a deep breath. "I can!" she said.

"Isn't this much better than riding past the flowers in the coach? We couldn't smell anything when we were cooped up in there."

"What a painting this would make!" Meg said. "I'm seeing a bed of green peppered with purple, orange, yellow and red! I wish I could have brought my easel!"

"So, you're okay?" Lena asked.

"I am! I like this. I do."

"I never would have thought that just a few months past our horrible birthday I would be this happy!" Lena said.

And, she added to herself, now that Meg and I can ride alone, we'll definitely make it to Palindrome Pond for our eleventh birthday!

Marcus and Fran smiled. They guided the horses to a spot where the grass was short, helped the girls off, and settled for their picnic.

"When did you come to this castle?" Marcus asked Fran during lunch.

"I came here the year before the girls were born."

"And, where did you come from?" Marcus asked.

"Another kingdom entirely. Far from here."

"What brought you here?" he asked.

Fran hesitated.

Lena stopped herself from blurting out, "Palindrome Pond!"

"I'll tell you some other time," Fran said.

Meg saw Marcus nod his head. It seemed to Meg that Marcus was trying to decide whether to ask Fran another question, or just accept that she didn't seem to want to talk to him.

"Can you tell us more about Clara?" Fran asked.

Meg smiled. Maybe Fran would let herself become friends with Marcus after all, she thought.

"I actually just received a letter from her. She has been riding frequently with my brothers."

"I want you to bring her here," said Lena. "I'm sure we could be friends."

"But, Lena, you know Mother and Father don't allow us visitors," said Meg.

"But, Clara is all grown up. Surely she wouldn't endanger or tease me. I'm certain Father would invite Clara here."

Marcus smiled. "I'm so pleased that you want to meet her," he said. "And, I'm sure she would love to meet you as well. She hasn't any friends. She spends all of her time with the family."

Marcus paused. He looked into the distance.

"Clara must miss you very much," Fran said.

"And, I miss her," Marcus said. He fell silent a moment. Then, he grinned. "But, what a wonderful time I am having with all of you!"

Fran smiled back.

"All right," she said. "Let's finish up and get back to the stables. We still have some lessons to finish today."

They packed up and retraced their way along the trail. As they rounded the final bend, Fran stopped. Invincible halted next to her.

"Why are we stopping?" Lena asked.

"Look," Fran said, pointing ahead.

In the distance, near the stables, stood a coach. Standing next to the coach were two people, draped in capes.

"Mother and Father!" Lena muttered. "They're back. They're already back!"

Chapter Twenty-Six

As the four neared the stables, the King came running toward them.

"What is this?" the King shouted as he rushed to them. "Be careful. Marcus! Fran! What is this? Girls, how can you be up there by yourselves?"

"We're fine!" Lena called. "We're happy up here!"

"Get them down!" the Queen ordered.

The King reached the foursome and glared at Marcus. "I never said to let her ride alone!" he said.

"My apologies, your majesty. I must have misunderstood," Marcus replied.

"But, we want to be up here, Father. We belong up here," Lena said.

"Get them down!" the Queen repeated.

"Get Lena down!" echoed the King.

"Wait until you see how Invincible helps me off! He's perfect for me!"

Meg dismounted with ease, handed the reins to Fran, and ran to her mother.

The Queen threw her arms around Meg, watching fearfully as Lena dismounted.

Marcus motioned for Invincible to kneel. Then, he lifted Lena off the horse's back.

"See!" Lena said. "I'm fine!"

The King reached for Lena and Marcus handed her over.

Lena hugged her father. "I know you wanted me to ride," she whispered in his ear. "I know you sent Marcus and Invincible to me. It's the best thing you could have ever done for me. I love you, Father."

The King cuddled Lena and walked toward the Queen who was hurrying in their direction.

"I'm fine, Mother," Lena said. "This is the best I've ever been."

"Fran! How could you permit this?" the Queen demanded as the King settled Lena in her chair.

Fran stood tall, her hands clutching one another in front of her body. "Your majesty," she curtsied, looking at the King.

"Fran did only what she thought I intended," the King said.

"What?" the Queen stared at her husband.

"This is Marcus, our new chief stable hand. Perhaps you recognize him from when we needed blacksmith assistance on our journey?" the King asked.

The Queen turned to Marcus. She stared at him. "I recall the blacksmith shop but I do not recognize this gentleman."

"When we arrived at the blacksmith shop, I saw him standing next to a horse. A young woman was walking toward him with jerky movements, bracing herself with a cane in each hand. When she reached him, he had the horse bow like we just saw Lena's horse do. Marcus lifted the woman onto the horse. He then mounted behind her and they took a ride."

"This woman—she was using canes because she had been injured?" the Queen asked.

Marcus shook his head.

"The woman, your majesty, is my sister, Clara. She was not injured. She always has had difficulty controlling her movements. Like Lena."

"Well, if she can walk, she isn't like Lena at all!" the Queen said.

Lena barely stopped herself from screaming. Her mother always made her feel worse. Lena didn't see how her mother would ever understand.

"My dear," the King said, "I talked to Marcus for quite some time while our horse was in his father's care. What I heard convinced me that we should let Lena try to ride—with Marcus on the horse at the same time."

"You sent Marcus here to teach Lena how to ride?" The Queen said through gritted teeth.

"I did," the King said. "But, I thought she would only ride with Marcus on the same horse, sitting behind her."

"Allow me to explain, your highness," Marcus said. "For more than a month I did ride on Invincible with Lena. She became quite skilled in handling him and she learned to sit tall on him without leaning against me at all. She also worked daily on her body strengthening exercises. I could tell she was growing stronger—probably in part because she was riding Invincible. I noticed that with my sister as well."

"But, your sister doesn't ride alone?" the Queen said.

"No. But she never has asked to. Lena—that's all she wants to do." He looked at the King. "Recalling, your majesty, that you instructed that I use my judgment…well…I decided to let her try."

"And I can do it!" Lena shouted. "I love it! And I'm finally happy!"

"Fran," said the Queen, turning to the nanny, "didn't you see the danger?"

"I'm not in danger, Mother!" Lena interrupted. "Did you see how slowly we were going? That's as fast as I've ever gone. There's no danger."

"You still could fall," the Queen said.

"Well, Meg fell once and she didn't get hurt!"

"You fell?" the Queen turned to Meg.

"I did," Meg answered. "And, it's true, I didn't get hurt. Just a little bruised. But, I was fine. It was good to fall, actually. It helped me not be afraid."

The King smiled.

"I think we're done for now," the King said. "Your mother and I will need to talk more about this in private."

"You'll let me keep riding, won't you?" Lena begged.

"Your father and I will discuss it," the Queen said.

"I'll die if I can't ride!" Lena said.

"You'll do no such thing," the Queen said.

"Lena, let your mother and me talk," the King interjected.

"And we shall talk about your continued employ, Marcus. And yours, Fran," the Queen added.

"You can't take them from us!" Lena shouted. "We need them!"

"Mother, please! Fran is family!" Meg said.

"We're going to discuss everything," the Queen said. "Now, it's time we went back to the castle."

Chapter Twenty-Seven

That night, the girls were silent through their bedtime ritual. Lavender bubble baths. Warmed towels to dry off. Silken dressing gowns. Hot tea and cookies at their bedside.

"Cookies," Lena frowned. "Who can think of cookies?"

Fran lifted Lena into bed. Meg climbed in beside her sister. Fran smoothed the fluffy comforter over the girls' limp bodies.

"Fran," Meg's voice cracked. "Do you think Mother and Father will send you away?"

"Please, don't worry about me." She gave each of them a tight hug.

"I wish there was something I could do," Lena said.

"You've done enough!" Meg cried.

Lena was startled. Meg never yelled at her. Meg never yelled at anyone.

"Meg, what's wrong?" she asked.

"Fran might have to leave—and it's your fault!"

"My fault? You're mad at *me*?"

"Yes! You knew Mother didn't want you to ride. She didn't even want you to touch a horse. But you had to have your way!"

"But Father made it possible. He sent Marcus to me!"

"But, you pushed to ride alone. Father didn't want that!"

"You wanted to ride alone, too!" Lena said.

"You made me want to!"

"I made you? How could I have made you?"

"You said you would learn to ride without me!"

"So? You paint without me."

"That's different. You could have waited, Lena!"

"Waited? I've been waiting my whole life! You don't know how it feels—not to be able to do anything without help."

"But, now we might lose Fran!" Meg cried.

"Hush, hush. Girls," Fran interrupted. "Please. We're all upset and concerned. I've never heard the two of you like this. Please. Stop."

Meg buried her face under the covers. Lena pushed herself so she lay on her side, facing away from Meg.

Fran sat next to Meg. "Shh...shh..." she said repeatedly, rubbing her back. "Everything will be all right....shh...shh."

"How can you say that?" Meg choked.

"Because, I have seen how life works," Fran comforted. "One thing leads to another...and...well, once you're there, you can't imagine it any other way."

"But, what if you don't like where it leads?" Meg asked, lifting her tear-streaked face from the embroidered pillow.

"At first, you may not like it. But, you find your way. You do, like I found my way to you."

"But, now they might send you away. Because of Lena!"

"Stop saying that, Meg! It's not my fault!"

"Girls, please. I am certain this will all work out."

"You'll probably marry Marcus and run off with him and leave us here," Meg said.

"I'll never leave if your parents will have me," Fran said. "I promise. Never. Now, get some sleep. Let's see what tomorrow brings."

Chapter Twenty-Eight

Meg couldn't sleep. She tossed and turned. Her stomach felt as twisted as a corkscrew. Finally, she slithered from under the covers. She had to talk to her parents. She needed Fran. Wasn't her happiness just as important as Lena's? She had to make them understand.

Meg leaned over to check Lena. She had never left her sister alone in the room. But, this was important. She wouldn't be gone long.

Meg stumbled as she felt her way to the door. Her small body cast dancing shadows along the torch-lit corridor to her parents' chamber.

The heavy oak door creaked as Meg entered. A single torch burning in their room showed they were sleeping soundly. She crawled onto her parents' bed, knelt between them, then shook each in turn.

"Father...Mother...please...wake up...I need to talk to you."

The Queen woke first. "Meg! What's wrong?"

That woke the King. He bolted up. "What? What happened? Is Lena all right?"

It's always about Lena, Meg thought. "Yes, she's fine. I need to talk to you."

"Very well," said the King.

"I know how upset you are with Fran and Marcus."

Meg took a deep breath. She'd never argued with her parents. The King nodded. Meg twisted her hands in her silk gown.

"I just need you to know, to understand, that I don't feel I could be happy without Fran." Meg searched for some sign in her parents' faces that they understood. But the flickering torchlight played across two blank faces, waiting for her to continue.

"It's just—well, we rode to make Lena happy. And, well, we all worry about Lena, but, it's just." Meg stumbled over her words. "It's just that—I want to be happy, too! And, I thought you should know what I want to be happy." That was all. She could think of nothing else to say.

Finally, the King spoke. "You go back to bed, sweet child. Fran can stay, but, later this morning we will discuss some new rules."

Meg flung herself at her parents. "Thank you! Thank you!" she cried, peppering them with hugs and kisses.

"Go back to bed, Meg," the King said, kissing his daughter's forehead.

Meg rushed back to her room and jumped in bed. She shook Lena awake. "I think Mother and Father are letting Fran stay!"

"How do you know?" Lena said, rubbing her eyes.

"I went to talk to them just now. I couldn't sleep."

Lena grabbed for her sister. "What a relief! What about Marcus?"

"I didn't ask about Marcus."

"You didn't? Why not?"

"I didn't think to."

"I need him to stay," Lena said. "Please, let him stay," she muttered.

Lena squeezed Meg's hand. "Are you still mad at me?"

"I guess not. But, Mother and Father are going to give us some new rules later. New rules, Lena." Meg said, tightening her grip around Lena's hand. "Whatever the new *rules* are, we have to obey them. Understand?"

Lena squeezed her hand and Meg thought that meant "yes." But Lena didn't say anything. Because no matter what her parents said, she wouldn't stop riding. Even if that meant running away, like Fran did. Maybe that's what Fran had seen in the pond. Maybe that was why Fran didn't want her to ride alone. Because Fran was afraid Lena might ride away forever. But it didn't matter. Lena was going to ride to Palindrome Pond on her eleventh birthday. And who knew where after that.

Chapter Twenty-Nine

The sun was high when the girls finally heard footsteps coming down the hallway. As the King and Queen entered their room, Lena reached for Meg's hand.

Please don't say you won't let me ride, thought Lena.

"We have spent considerable time talking with each other—and with Marcus," the King said. "We felt we needed to hear more from him about the riding, and how each of you is doing with it."

"Can I keep riding?" blurted Lena, unable to stand the suspense.

"Be patient, Lena," the King said, seating himself on the bed next to Lena. "We have made many decisions. They are not to be debated. Listen well.

"First, Fran and Marcus will remain at the castle."

"Marcus, too? Oh, thank you! Thank you!" Lena said.

"This does not mean that we approve of how things were handled. We do understand how Marcus misinterpreted my wishes. And, we believe that he and Fran are most able to care for you. Lena, they know your physical abilities far better than we. We fear that it would be irresponsible to release them without having others to replace them."

"No one could ever replace them," Lena insisted.

"Can't you just listen?" Meg nudged Lena.

"Second, we will permit you to continue to ride."

"Yes!" cried Lena. She hugged her father. "Thank you! Thank you."

"From what Marcus has told us, it seems the riding is good for you—body and spirit. Still, this does not mean that you can ride whenever and wherever you'd like."

We'll see about that, Lena thought.

"Can I ride on Invincible by myself? Did Marcus tell you that I've been riding alone for almost a month? And that I've never had a problem? And that Invincible obeys me? And that I know what I'm doing?"

"Slow down, Lena," the King said. "Yes, he told us everything. We still prefer that he or Fran ride on Invincible with you, but we aren't insisting that they do. We do want one of them to continue to walk alongside you. And, we forbid you directing Invincible to walk any faster than he has been. There will be no trotting at all. Do you understand?"

"I do, Father. Of course."

The Queen took in a breath so loud, it caught Lena's attention. Lena looked at her mother who appeared to be fighting tears. Why? Lena wondered. Because she had given in to the King? Or because she actually was afraid Lena might be harmed? Lena realized she didn't understand her mother at all. But right now, she was just grateful that her mother had agreed to what she wanted. That was a start in the right direction.

"Finally, no more spending all day at the stables. You have to study. And you need to do so in a study space, not a horse barn.

"And, we will map out where you are and are not permitted to ride within the castle grounds. You remain forbidden to leave the castle area.

"If these rules are broken, we will punish you. And, if Fran or Marcus breaks any rule, we will send them away."

Lena nodded. "I'm sure Fran and Marcus will never break a rule," she said.

And as long as Palindrome Pond is one of Father's permitted destinations, I won't either, she thought.

Chapter Thirty

As the girls' eleventh birthday approached, Lena began to plot her trip to Palindrome Pond. She knew she couldn't involve Fran or Marcus. She didn't want them to be fired. She was willing to go alone, but hoped that Meg would come with her. It would be hard for Lena to get on Invincible and go alone. Still, she thought it best to wait to tell her sister until the last minute—so Meg didn't have time to think of all the reasons not to go.

They'd sneak off after their birthday visit to the village. The Queen said it was now their royal duty to participate in the journey each year. The rules were the same this year as for their tenth—no getting out of the coach. No contact with the villagers. Lena didn't complain. She would just go along for the ride, without objection. Knowing that her trip to the pond would follow later that afternoon, Lena thought she could handle anything. Besides, it would give her a chance to watch for landmarks along the path to the village, and that should make the trip to Palindrome Pond much easier.

On the morning of their eleventh birthday, Lena was awake as always before the sunrise. She jostled her sister.

"Meg, wake up, wake up."

Meg groaned.

"It's our birthday! Our palindrome birthday!" Lena said.

Meg rubbed her eyes. "Yes, Lena. Happy Birthday." She rolled over and buried her face in the pillow.

"Meg, listen. Listen up. We're going to Palindrome Pond today!"

"Really?" Meg sat up. "When was that decided?"

"I decided ages ago. Remember?"

"You mean, before all the new rules?"

"Yes."

"So, are you telling me that Mother and Father have decided to take us to the pond today? Instead of in the coach to the village for our birthday?"

"No, Meg! They don't even know about the pond. At least, I don't think they do."

"So, then, who said we could go?"

"No one. But no one said we *couldn't* go either."

"Lena," Meg said, shaking her head. "You know that leaving the castle grounds is forbidden."

"Meg, we have to go today. If we don't we won't be able to visit the pond until we are twenty-two! We can't wait that long!"

"I can."

"Well, I can't. And I'm going today, whether you come along or not. Invincible will take care of me."

"Invincible?"

"I have a plan. A perfect plan. And, we have Fran's map—the copy that you made."

"Lena—we can't do this! Fran and Marcus will get fired!"

"Not if they don't know we're going! That way, they won't be part of breaking any more rules. It has to be just us—or just me."

Meg buried her face in her hands. "You know I'd never let you go alone." She shook her head. "Just when do you plan on doing this?"

"After we get back from the village. Mother and Father already have said we can take a birthday ride on the horses—it's perfect!"

"Perfectly crazy," Meg said. "This is going to be trouble."

Chapter Thirty-One

"Happy birthday, girls!" Fran sang as she entered the room. "And, what a glorious day it is. The sky is its richest blue and not a cloud in sight!"

Meg frowned. "I'm scared," she whispered to Lena. "And, you should be too."

Fran approached the bed. "Are you feeling upset about the trip to the village this year?"

"Not really," Lena said. "I know what to expect. And, I get to ride Invincible later, right?"

"Of course. Marcus will have Invincible and Jackson ready," Fran said. "I'll be waiting for you. When you return, we'll change your clothes and go for a great ride!"

She helped the girls slip into this year's new birthday dresses—sea blue taffeta with crystal beading. She placed the tiaras on the princesses' heads.

I don't know why we are wearing these special clothes, Lena thought. It's not as if anyone other than Mother and Father will see them.

Sir and Ruby were pulling the coach again. All along the way, Lena studied the trail, looking for clues that would help her find Palindrome Pond. At the village square, Lena looked at the villagers with new eyes. She wondered whether they would tease her. Whether they would be afraid of her. Were Father and Fran right? She'd get to the pond. Then she'd figure out how to meet the villagers. Then, she would find out for herself what they thought of her.

Upon returning home, the King and Queen thanked the girls for a pleasant trip and wished them an enjoyable ride.

"We'll see you at dinner," the Queen said. "Don't forget, there'll be presents!"

Lena could tell her mother was pleased that the journey had gone smoothly this year.

The Queen retired for a nap and the King met with his advisors.

Lena was practically sweating by the time Fran finally came to help them change into riding clothes. She was desperate to get on their way.

Marcus greeted them at the stables with Invincible and Jackson already saddled.

"Invincible!" Lena called. She stretched out her arms as Fran wheeled her next to the horse. Invincible neighed softly and nuzzled Lena with his velvety striped nose.

"Marcus, can you help me mount right away? I can't wait," said Lena.

Marcus laughed, then settled Lena on Invincible.

Lena's stomach started fluttering. This was going to be the tricky part.

"Oh, Marcus," she said, as innocently as possible, "will you go to the tack room and get Invincible's brushes so I can groom him when we rest on our ride?"

"Certainly," Marcus replied.

"Thank you." Lena waited for Marcus to turn the corner of the barn, then said, "Oh, Fran, I forgot. There's that blanket in the tack room, the one I like to sit on during our breaks. Could you run get it? Meg can stay with me."

"Certainly," Fran said.

As Fran headed toward the barn, Lena motioned to Meg. "Quick," she said. "Go lock Marcus and Fran in the tack room! Hurry!"

Meg raced after Fran. She peered into the barn and saw Fran enter the tack room. Heart pounding, she darted to the door, slammed it shut and bolted it.

"Hey," Marcus yelled, banging on the door. "Who did that? What's happening?"

"Lena! Meg!" Fran cried with panic in her voice. "Are you okay?"

Meg couldn't bear for them to worry.

"Don't worry," Meg called through the thick wooden door. "Lena and I are fine. It's just that Lena insists on going to Palindrome Pond and we couldn't let you break any more rules. So, we're locking you in here until we get back."

Meg took a deep breath. "I can't let Lena go alone," she said, laying her hands on the door. "Please don't be mad at us."

"Let us out," Marcus said sternly. "Where are you going? Where?"

"Meg, no!" Fran cried. "Not the pond!"

Meg backed away from the door.

"I have to help Lena," Meg said. "I promise, we'll be careful. We made a copy of your map, Fran. It's not that far away. We'll be back soon."

As Meg returned to Lena she heard Fran's faint call from behind the door…"careful"…"water"…"don't lean too far."

"What took you so long?" Lena asked impatiently.

"I locked them in and then I explained," Meg said, swiping at her forehead.

"Meg, what if they break out? They'll try to come and stop us."

"Lena, is that all you care about?" Meg slammed her fist in the palm of the other hand. "They love us. They worry about us. Why make this any harder on them than it has to be? Just be grateful I'm helping you. I probably shouldn't!"

Lena knew Meg was right, but, she didn't want to miss this one chance in eleven years to see the future. She swallowed hard. "I'm sorry, Meg. I am grateful. I am. Please, get on Jackson. Let's go."

Meg gave her sister a stern glance as she swung into the saddle.

"I have a bad feeling," Meg said as they walked the horses toward the main gate. "Fran was shouting something as I left. It sounded like she was really scared about us going to the pond. Remember how shaken she was from her last trip there?"

Lena's stomach flopped. She recalled Mr. Stuts saying something about telling them too soon. And, Fran saying something about someone looking dead. But, how could that have anything to do with her? And, how could she resist seeing her future? They would go, just as she had planned.

"We'll be extra careful," Lena said as they approached the main gate. "Nothing bad is going to happen."

Chapter Thirty-Two

"Good afternoon!" Lena called to the patrol guarding the gate. "Isn't this a beautiful day for our birthday and for our special ride?"

The guard lowered his sword. He looked puzzled. "Good afternoon, Your Highnesses. And, Happy Birthday. Indeed, it is a beautiful day. But, I know nothing about a special ride."

"Well, we have been planning this special birthday ride for months!"

The guard looked all around him. "Where's Fran? Why isn't she with you?"

"We wanted to spend some time alone on our birthday." Lena said.

The guard looked worried. "Begging your pardon, but the King..."

Lena put on her haughtiest voice. "My father knows our desires. Open the gate. I command you."

"If the King were only here to confirm..." the guard continued.

"Must we trample on you?" Lena said with exasperation. "This is our *birthday*," she said with force. "Move aside."

Lena clicked her tongue against her teeth and Invincible moved forward. Jackson followed.

"Open the gate!" Lena directed.

Hesitantly, the guard swung the heavy wooden gates open.

The girls rode in silence for a few minutes.

Meg's stomach was twisting.

"Father probably will fire that guard," Meg frowned. "We should go back."

"Oh, no! We're out! We have to go now. And, we have to get there before sunset, or we won't be able to see any reflections in the pond."

The girls rode on. "Meg, take out the map. We need to look it over."

Meg halted Jackson to study the map. She didn't want to make any wrong turns. "Okay," she said pointing. "Here's our castle. Here's the road we are on," her finger tracing the curvy line. According to this, we will take the third right turn. Then, the first left...Then, the second right. That should lead us there."

They rode on.

"I still have a bad feeling about this," Meg said, after the second turn took them onto a narrow path hemmed in by tall trees.

"We're so close," Lena said. "We have to keep going. Just one more turn!"

The trail narrowed even further when they made the last turn.

"This is it!" Lena said. "Soon, we should see trees with palindromes carved into them!"

They rode on.

"Oh no!" Meg said, as they came to a fork in the road. "That's not on the map!"

Meg thought back to the night she copied Fran's map. "Lena—remember how I copied the map by candlelight?"

Lena nodded.

"Well, it was so dim I missed this. Or maybe it wasn't on the original. We'll have to turn back," she said, relieved.

"No! Never!" Lena said. "We'll pick one way and ride for ten minutes. If we don't see trees carved with palindromes, we'll turn around and take the other path."

Meg stared at Lena. "Fine," she said. "You choose—which way first?"

"Let's go right—maybe it will be the right way," Lena said.

But it wasn't. The bark on the trees was smooth and untouched.

So they retraced their steps and headed down the other path.

Within a hundred paces they spied the first palindrome. "'I saw I was I.'"

"It's just like the diary said!" cried Lena. "We're almost there!"

The trees had become denser. "That tree says 'Hannah'," Lena said. "A palindrome name!"

"And that one says 'No trace, not one carton!'" Meg pointed.

Nearly every tree bore a palindrome—single words, phrases, numbers, even math equations.

It was dim amongst the trees, and the girls had to squint to decipher many of the palindromes. The trail took a sharp turn at "I mad, Am I?" A few paces in front of them the path widened into a small clearing. Wide sunbeams streamed down.

"The clearing!" Lena said. "Just as Stovall described!"

Silvery white sand surrounding a crystal clear pool of water. Water so calm it appeared to be a plate of glass.

Lena and Meg nudged their mounts to the very edge of the water.

The horses' reflections stared back at them.

Chapter Thirty-Three

"Meg, I think you'll have to help me down so I can see my reflection. I'll only see Invincible in the pond as long as I'm up here," Lena said.

Meg dismounted and tied Jackson's reins around a tree. She had Invincible kneel, then reached under Lena's arms, as she had seen Marcus do dozens of times.

Meg hesitated. "Lena, I can help you slide off, but I don't think I could get you back on."

"What are you talking about?" Lena asked impatiently.

"You're heavy! Fran and Marcus usually lift you. I don't think I can!"

In her frustration, Lena yanked on Invincible's reins. Taking that as his cue to rise, he heaved upward. The horse struggled to regain his footing, taking several steps into the pond. Lena lurched forward, off balance, flailing wildly. The air whooshed from her lungs as she thumped hard onto Invincible's withers. Lena slid her arms around the horse's neck and lay there panting as Meg rushed to steady her.

"This was a bad idea, Lena. We're going home, now!"

Frightened more than she wanted to admit, Lena was about to agree when she opened her eyes. She was lying forward, along Invincible's neck—and she could see down into the water.

"Meg," she whispered. "I can see myself."

"What?"

"I can see myself."

Meg started talking again, but Lena tuned her out.

Taking a deep breath, she slowly recited the palindrome from the old map. "Are we not drawn onward, we few, drawn onward to new era?"

At once, gentle ripples flowed through the water.

Then, the water surface returned to utter calm.

"Meg! Look!"

"What? I only see you and Invincible!"

"I see us! I see me doing my exercises in the sunroom—you are holding my feet. And, I see Father taking me to meet the horse for the first time. And, now I see Mother and Father riding off in the coach. There we are at the stables—with Marcus and Fran! We're riding!" Lena's heart was pounding.

"The past!" Meg said. She wondered why she couldn't see it, too.

"I don't see any more pictures!" Lena said. "That's it? I want to see more!"

"Look!" Meg said, "The water is shifting!"

The water rippled in the other direction. Then, returned to calm.

"Anything now?" Meg asked.

"Yes!" Lena cried. "I see children. So many children. Some are running. Some are in chairs—like mine! Like mine, Meg! Some are walking with canes. Oh—now I see children on horses—and, and, children painting! And there we are!"

"What else?" Meg asked.

"The pictures are fading." Lena sighed. "That went so fast! But, they were amazing. Amazing!" She pulled herself upright on Invincible.

"It's your turn, Meg. You look in!"

"No, let's go," Meg said, walking towards Jackson.

"But, Meg, you're here. You have to look."

"What if I see something scary, like Fran did last time?"

"Well, then we should find out about it—so we can make choices to stop it."

Meg sighed. "If I look, can we go?"

"Of course!"

Meg stepped to the water's edge. Quietly, she said, "Are we not drawn onward, we few, drawn onward to new era?"

"The water's rippling!" Lena said. Then it was calm.

"Oh!" Meg said. "I see us at the stables, too. I see you on Invincible and me watching from the ground. Now I am painting…and riding Jackson with Fran…and now alone."

The images faded as quickly as they had appeared. "That was fast," Meg remarked.

The water rippled the other way.

"What now?" Lena said.

"I see the children! Just like you said, Lena. I see them on horses, and some of them painting! Lena, either the spring can't tell us apart, or we have the same future!"

Eager to see the image again, Lena leaned toward the pond. But she was already too low on Invincible's neck. She slipped over Invincible's side and plunged into the water.

Chapter Thirty-Four

Invincible neighed wildly, his stomping hooves churning up mud at the water's edge.

Meg surged into the water yelling.

"Lena! Lena!"

Lena's entire body was submerged. She flapped her arms, splashing water in every direction. She managed to propel her head out of the water, yelp a garbled "Help!," only to sink again.

Meg was in the water waist high, but could barely step forward. Was there quicksand on the pond's floor? She heaved one leg at a time, finally reaching Lena.

"Lift your head!" Meg cried, thrusting her arms into the water. She grabbed Lena's neck and pulled her sister's face above surface.

Lena sputtered as Meg struggled to support her.

"You're choking me!" croaked Lena.

Meg let go, and Lena slipped underwater again.

"No!" cried Meg.

She grabbed Lena. This time, she managed to hook her arms under her sister's armpits. Meg hauled Lena to the surface again.

Lena wheezed, trying to catch her breath. She could feel the blood pounding fiercely through her body.

Meg panted along with her. How were they going to get out? She could barely manage to keep her balance and support Lena's head above water. The sandy bottom surely would suck them both down if she tried to move.

Meg looked at Invincible and then at Jackson. They both seemed miles away. Invincible dropped his head and his reins fell into the pond. He neighed and shook his head from side to side. His reins floated in the water.

That's it! Meg thought. If I can coax him farther into the water, close to me, I can grab his reins and he can pull us out.

Meg called to him. She clucked her tongue against the roof of her mouth. "Invincible, come."

He didn't move—just stared at the girls in the water and neighed.

"Invincible...come! Come here Invincible!"

At last the horse responded. He splashed forward and made his way slowly to the girls as Meg continued calling to him.

"Good boy! Wonderful boy, Invincible!" Meg said when he reached them.

"Lena, you're going to have to help. Put your arms around my neck and hold on. Hold on tight!"

Keeping one arm securely around her sister, Meg grabbed Invincible's trailing reins. "Take us to shore, Invincible. Pull us out boy."

The horse didn't move. He looked at Meg, as if trying to understand.

"Back Invincible! Back!" muttered Lena.

The horse responded immediately and backed toward the bank, towing the princesses with him. Meg's hands burned as she gripped his reins.

Invincible clambered out of the pond, pulling the bedraggled princesses onto the silvery sand.

Breathless, Meg collapsed into the tiny crystals and turned her head to look at her sister. She wiped away soaked strands of hair that covered her eyes. Lena's drenched body was splayed next to her, eyes closed.

"Lena!" No answer. As she reached to shake her twin, Invincible edged toward Lena and lowered his nose toward the princess. Cool water dripped from his muzzle onto her pale face.

Lena flinched. Then she coughed, retching up water.

Meg struggled to her knees. She grabbed both of Lena's arms, dragged her away from the pond's edge then sat with her back to her sister, head in hands, weeping.

"Meg," Lena murmured, reaching out a shaky hand to her twin.

"Lena, you could have died!" Meg pounded her fists into the powdery sand.

Lena lifted her head. "Meg...I'm...I'm so sorry."

"I should never have agreed to this," Meg cried.

"I'm sorry," Lena said. "I'm sorry."

The sun had sunk low in the western sky and the trees cast long shadows across the clearing. Meg was shivering. She could see that Lena was too.

"Meg, I want to go home."

"Lena. I can't lift you, remember? I can't get you back on Invincible."

"You can ride. You go get help."

"No. I'm not going to leave you alone. We'll have to wait for someone to find us."

Both girls were quiet then, lost in their own thoughts as the shadows lengthened.

It was Lena who broke the silence. "I know!" she said. "You can't lift me, but, you can drag me, Meg. Just drag me onto Invincible's back."

"What do you mean?"

"Just flop me over him on my stomach. I can ride that way."

Meg sighed. "It's worth a try."

Invincible was still standing by Lena. Meg directed him to kneel. Then, with the horse between her and Lena, she reached over, grabbed Lena's wrists, and pulled. And pulled. Little by little she lugged her sister across the horse's back.

"Perfect!" Lena said. "Now, raise your arm up, Meg, for Invincible to rise."

With Invincible standing, Meg could see that Lena actually was quite secure in that position.

"Thank you, Meg," Lena said, her voice muffled against Invincible's side.

"Lena, I can maneuver you around now that you're up there. Maybe even help you sit up."

Lena hated to admit it, but she didn't have the strength to keep herself upright. She didn't even have the strength to hold on.

She told Meg to leave her where she was.

Lena was shaking so hard Meg thought she must be very cold. But then she heard the sobs Lena was trying to suppress. Lena—fierce, determined, stubborn Lena—was crying. Meg's anger dissolved and she reached to her sister awkwardly.

"I love you. Let's go home."

Chapter Thirty-Five

Meg and Jackson led the way. Invincible dutifully followed at their side, his reins joined with Jackson's in Meg's hands. The girls' drenched clothes, caked with sand, clung to their bodies. Neither spoke.

As they turned onto the main road, they heard a steady thundering, getting closer.

Peering into the gloom, Meg saw men on horses led by her father, his crimson cape streaming behind him as he rushed toward them. As the gap between the two parties narrowed, Meg saw his eyes focused on Lena's body sprawled across Invincible, limp and sagging, looking like a corpse.

"We're all right," Meg called, trying to reassure him. But he did not slow his pace.

When he reached them, the King vaulted from the saddle and ran to Lena. He lifted her head in his shaking hands.

"I'm okay, Father," Lena sobbed, shivering.

He patted Invincible and pulled Lena into his arms, then looked at Meg.

"You're okay?" he asked.

She nodded.

"What happened?"

141

"It's a long story. Can we just go home?"

He agreed, saying only, "There will be a reckoning when we get there."

As they entered the castle grounds, Marcus came running. The King surrendered Lena to him, then dismounted. Holding Lena's limp bedraggled body in his arms, Marcus walked toward the castle where Fran and Mr. Stuts stood watching.

Fran grabbed Mr. Stuts' arm. "That's it," she gasped. "The very image I saw in the pond. We weren't able to prevent it after all."

The King helped Meg off Jackson. He hugged her tightly. The King told one of his gentry to take special care of the horses. "They've been through an ordeal of some kind," he said.

The King's words went right to Lena's heart. She had put everyone through an ordeal—everyone who cared for her, including Invincible.

Mr. Stuts approached Lena. "You are all right?" he asked, his eyes welling with tears.

As Lena reached to him, her hand slipped and caught in the collar of his shirt. She jerked her hand up and a gold chain flipped out of Mr. Stuts' clothing. A shiny gold pendant hung from it.

Lena held it in her hand. It was the symbol! Palindrome Pond!

Lena looked into Mr. Stuts' eyes. "Who is the Stuts in Stovall's diary?" she asked.

"It is I," Mr. Stuts replied.

"You?" Lena said. "But, that diary seems ancient."

"As am I," said the librarian.

"Mr. Stuts told me how to find the pond," the King said. "But, I've yet to hear what it is all about."

"When you wish, Sir, I shall explain," Mr. Stuts said.

"Are you allowed to?" Lena asked the librarian.

"I can do whatever I wish in regard to the Society. It is I who created it."

"But, how did you even know about the pond?"

"I was present when it was created."

When was that? Lena wondered. Just how old was Mr. Stuts? And who was he, really? Lena had so many more questions. But, just then, the Queen dashed out of the castle and ran to her family.

"My girls," she called.

She ran to Lena first, who was still nestled in Marcus' arms. She kissed her forehead and caressed her tangled hair. Lena looked into her mother's eyes. She saw fear and relief. She saw love. She saw her mother's love.

The Queen turned to Meg. She grabbed her and held her, kissing the top of Meg's head as it pressed against her chest.

Marcus put Lena in her chair.

Looking past her frowning father, Lena called to Fran and Marcus. "How did you get out of the tack room?"

"Mr. Stuts came to the stables with some knights. They heard us pounding on the door and let us out," Fran said.

"Mr. Stuts?" Lena asked. She turned to him. "How did you know?"

"I trembled," he replied.

"You trembled?" Lena said.

"Yes. Perhaps you recall my trembling in the library on Fran's birthday?"

"I do!" Meg said.

"My left side trembles whenever someone invokes the magic of the pond," Mr. Stuts said.

"What is this about?" the Queen demanded.

"Apparently," said the King, "all will be revealed to us. First, the girls should get cleaned up. Then, we shall meet…and punishments will be levied."

Chapter Thirty-Six

Bathed and dressed, the girls and Fran joined the King, Queen, Marcus and Mr. Stuts in the sitting room.

Lena was anxious to learn her punishment. She had her own idea of what it might be.

Lena jumped right in. "Fran and Marcus had nothing to do with our trip," she said. "It was all my plan. Punish me. Only me."

"And, what do you see as apt punishment?" asked the King.

"I think I shouldn't be allowed to ride Invincible for a month," she suggested.

The King nodded. "Let's make it three. But, you'll continue to do your exercises," he added. "And, you'll do that work here. Not at the stables."

Lena dared not argue. She looked down. "Father," she said, "won't Invincible be lonely not seeing me for so long?"

"Marcus can bring him by occasionally for you to say hello."

Lena smiled.

The King turned to Meg.

"I know you have to punish me, too," she said. "I should never have agreed to Lena's plan."

The King shook his head. "That's right, you shouldn't have." He sighed. "What would you have done differently, Meg?"

"I would have told Fran and Marcus everything," she said. "We would have kept Lena from going to the pond."

The King nodded. "That would have been wise, indeed." He paused. "Meg, you are also banned from riding for three months."

"And," the Queen said, "we will not be handing out birthday gifts tonight."

"Now," said the King, "about this pond. It is time to tell all."

"Majesties," said Mr. Stuts, bowing. "Permit me to inform."

Mr. Stuts described the pond's workings in precise detail.

When he finished, the Queen was the first to speak. Lena was amazed that her mother's first words were not a reprimand, but, rather, a question.

"Lena, did the pond's magic work for you?"

Lena nodded.

"What did you see?" her mother asked.

"Meg and I saw the same thing," Lena said in a hopeful tone. "So many children, Mother…Here. Here at the castle. They were riding horses. And painting. Some were in chairs, like mine," Lena said.

"And," Meg added, "some were using canes—probably like Marcus' sister, Clara."

"And, some children were running," Lena said.

The Queen nodded. Lena could see that her mother was thinking—thinking deeply. Lena dared not utter another word.

At last, the Queen spoke again.

"It sounds like your life purpose is to touch the lives of others," she said.

Lena's eyes grew wide. "I would like that…so, so much."

The Queen paused. She looked at the King, then spoke. "Why don't you start with Clara?"

"Clara?" Lena asked, confused. She looked at Marcus who was grinning. Her mother couldn't possibly mean what she was saying.

"Yes, Clara," the Queen said. "Marcus, at the conclusion of the girls' punishment, please arrange for your sister to visit. We would like to know her."

"Most happily, your majesty," Marcus bowed.

Lena couldn't believe it. Had her mother's attitude really changed? Would it last? It seemed too good to be true. After all these years of fighting, begging for any opportunity to meet new people, was the fighting over?

"Thank you, Mother," Lena finally said. "Thank you."

The Queen nodded at Lena and smiled.

Lena turned to Mr. Stuts. She wanted to know so much more about him and Palindrome Pond.

"How old *are* you?" she asked.

"I stopped counting long ago," Mr. Stuts replied.

"You said you were present when the pond was created," Meg said. "Who created it?"

"Ah...an invisible power greater than all of us," he replied.

"A *magical* power?" Lena asked.

"You could say so," said Mr. Stuts.

"Do you have magical powers?" Lena asked.

"Not exactly," he replied. "I like to describe myself as a being of wisdom and truth...though, I have seen that even I can allow passion to override wisdom."

"You mean because you told us about the pond?" Meg asked.

"Indeed," Mr. Stuts replied. "I brought you into the Society before you were ready."

"But, you had planned to bring us in...eventually?" Lena asked.

Mr. Stuts nodded. "Most certainly." He reached into his pocket and pulled out two chains, each with a dangling golden charm.

"The Palindrome Pond symbol!" Meg cried out.

Mr. Stuts approached each princess and placed one of the chains around her neck. "I wasn't expecting to present these to you for many years," he chuckled. "No sense keeping them hidden away any longer."

Lena lifted the charm off her chest and studied it. "Is this supposed to be a cylinder? To hold water from the pond?"

"That would have been clever, wouldn't it?" Mr. Stuts replied. "No, I'm afraid it's much simpler than that. I just drew two 'Ps', for 'Palindrome Pond', and I turned one of them upside down and then interlocked them."

"Just like it said in Stovall's diary!" exclaimed Meg.

Lena stared at the charm. "And, you always meant for us to have them?" she asked. "Truly?"

Mr. Stuts nodded. "Truly. I've always sensed that you, Lena, in particular, were someone who earnestly wished to discover your life purpose."

Lena smiled. "Well, I still don't understand why eleven is too young," she said.

"I never envisioned children as Pond Society members," Mr. Stuts offered. "New members never have been inducted until they have reached adulthood. Again, it's really quite simple. Adults are more likely to have the self-knowledge required to assess what they see in the pond and make wise choices to further their life purpose."

"But," said Lena. "I can make wise life choices."

"Like sneaking off to the pond without any grown-up to help you?" Mr. Stuts said.

Lena's shoulders sagged. "I see what you mean."

Mr. Stuts shook his head. "We almost lost you, Lena."

"But you didn't!" Lena protested. "Everything worked out fine."

She looked at Meg, who gazed back at her with raised eyebrows.

"Well, maybe not fine," she said. "I know it was a dangerous thing to do."

Marcus crouched down and looked into Lena's eyes.

"You're strong, Lena," he said with a smile. "But, are you invincible?"

Epilogue

On their twelfth birthday ride, the Queen surprised the princesses again. When the coach rounded the semi-circle formed by the villagers, the Queen motioned for the driver to stop. She disembarked and approached a young boy who sat in a wheeled chair in the front row of the crowd. Lena and Meg were riveted. The Queen bent down to his level, held his hand, and said something to him. The girls saw him nod his head and smile. They could see their mother grin from the moment she turned to face them.

"That was Rupert," the Queen announced as the King assisted her into the coach. "It appears that he would be most pleased to pay a visit to the castle to meet our lovely daughters…and perhaps to see if he might be able to ride a horse."

"Oh! Mother! Incredible! Thank you!" Lena bounced up and down on her bench. Meg smiled wide and hugged Lena. The King embraced his wife and waved to Rupert whose face was bright as sunshine. The girls leaned out their windows and waved vigorously to the crowd.

"Clara can help us with Rupert," said Meg. Clara now resided at the castle and was a frequent riding companion of the princesses.

Soon, children and their families from across the Kingdom came to visit the castle. Marcus began to teach other children how to ride horses. He eventually had an entire staff devoted to this effort.

Meg offered painting lessons to anyone who wished.

Fran helped supervise all of the activities.

One day, Lena sat in her chair overlooking the riding ring.

"Meg!" she called as her sister walked by holding freshly washed paintbrushes. "Look! I see children. So many children. Some are in chairs—like mine. Some are walking with canes. Some are on horses. Some are painting. Palindrome Pond was right about our future, Meg!"

Meg smiled. "Trust in the power of the palindrome."

"Yes," Lena said. "Trust in the power of the palindrome."

Lena looked at her twin. "I wonder," she said. "What mystery will the pond reveal when we are twenty two?"

ThE ENd

Afterword

By Christopher Reeve Foundation
www.christopherreeve.org

Chances are that, at some point in your life, you will be part of a family in which someone has a disability. It might be a temporary disability, like a broken leg. Or, it might be a permanent impairment, like the Christopher Reeve family experienced when Chris became paralyzed below his neck as a result of a spinal cord injury in a horseback riding accident.

Chris loved horses, and he would have loved that a horse gives Princess Lena the life for which she hoped. Actually, Chris, too, lived the life for which he hoped. He wanted to live a life that made a difference. He was a talented performing arts professional whose "life purpose" shifted when he was injured. He continued to write, produce, direct and act. But, he became much more than a performing arts professional. He became a champion for spinal cord medical research and for helping people with disabilities live better lives. Mostly, he became an inspiration to people all over the world to face their life challenges and to make the most of any situation, just like Princess Lena.

Chris wrote two books. The first is called *Still Me*. The second is called *Nothing is Impossible*. A third could have been called *Invincible*. That book might have been about the whole Reeve family; together, they were and are an invincible team. They learned, like Princesses Lena and Meg, the King and Queen, and Fran and Marcus, to battle fears, to discover new meaning in life, and to help each other grow through hardship.

In *Nothing Is Impossible*, Chris wrote:

> At some time, often when we least expect it, we all
> have to face overwhelming challenges. We are more
> troubled than we have ever been before. We may
> doubt that we have what it takes to endure. It is very
> tempting to give up, yet we have to find the will to
> keep going. But even when we discover what moti-
> vates us, we realize that we can't go the distance
> alone.

When the King and Queen learned that Lena, their daughter, couldn't walk, they faced an overwhelming challenge that
they didn't know how to manage. Meg grew up accepting a life
of isolation and caring for her twin. Lena felt they all had given
up. Her will pushed the whole family to grow. Together, they
discovered that they could change not only their lives, but
countless others. Wouldn't it be wonderful to spend time at
their castle, horseback riding, painting, and getting to know
all the families who visit? We, at the Christopher Reeve
Foundation hope that Lena and Meg will inspire you to see
people with disabilities for their Abilities. Take the time to get
to know them, be kind and welcoming, and let them get to
know you. After all, whatever your "life purpose" may be, you
can't go the distance alone.

Therapeutic Horseback Riding Afterword

By Nicoline Beveridge, Certified Therapeutic Horseback Riding Instructor, Washington, DC.

In the real world, would Lena be able to ride a horse? She most certainly would. All over the world, people of all ages with different disabilities ride everyday.

Who Can Ride?

Therapeutic riding students are people of all ages, varying from pre-schoolers to the elderly. They also have a wide range of disabilities, including physical, emotional, learning, and developmental. There are some who should not ride, because they are so fragile that they cannot risk falling and injuring themselves. The therapeutic riding instructor carefully evaluates every potential rider to determine that riding will be a beneficial and safe activity.

Why Ride?

Riding is a fun way to exercise both body and mind. There are doctors and physical therapists who recommend horseback riding for their patients. Being on top of a moving horse helps anyone develop better balance and stronger muscles. Those students who gain their own control over an animal as big as a horse develop important independence and leadership skills as well. There are people who can ride very well, even though they cannot walk. Imagine how empowering riding can be for someone who needs help from others for the simplest daily needs.

Special Equipment and Assistance

All riders must wear a helmet in case of a fall. There are different kinds of saddles or pads with handles, depending on the rider's needs. The instructor also may decide to have a horse leader and side aides for assistance. The horse leader helps to control the horse. Side aides can physically hold the rider in place, if that is necessary.

Selecting a Horse

Horses who work with therapeutic riding students must be calm, not easily scared, unconcerned with an off-balance or actively moving rider, and tolerant of being surrounded by a group of people (instructor, horse leader, and side aides). There are horses with a smooth walk, trot, and canter and those with bouncy gaits. Different horses work best with different people. There are plenty of therapeutic riders whose horse should stay at a walk or, at most, do a short trot. This means that older horses who are retired from racing or other strenuous activities can often start a whole new career as therapy partners.

Training a Horse

Most horses are highly trainable and adaptable to a variety of settings. It is critical that therapeutic riding horses learn to be comfortable with the types of sound, sight, and touch they are likely to encounter in the lesson. For instance, the horse must be familiar with a disabled rider's equipment, such as wheelchairs, crutches, or hearing aids that may start to whistle loudly when a connection fails. This is why Marcus insisted on carrying Lena into the stables the first time she met Invincible; he knew that the wheelchair and its noises might upset the horses initially.

Horses learn to trust that the activities of the riding lesson will not hurt them. Students may play games that involve blowing bubbles to help with breath control or throwing and catching balls to improve eye-hand coordination. Therapy horses are trained not to worry about incidences such as soap bubbles popping against their ears or balls bouncing off their rump and rolling between their legs.

Riding as a Sport

Many disabled riders become skilled enough to compete in horseback riding as a sport. Some compete with able-bodied riders. Others compete in shows for people with special needs. There are small, local competitions as well as large national and international events, including the Special Olympics and the Paralympics.

A famous competitive disabled rider, who competed in two Olympic Games, was a Danish woman named Lis Hartel. In 1944, she became infected with the polio virus, causing her to lose control over her arms and legs. Much like Lena, she was determined to make her body as strong and able as possible. She worked hard to re-train her arm and leg muscles. Once she was able to crawl, she started to work her way up to using crutches.

Three years later, Lis still did not have full use of her legs. This did not keep her from riding in the Scandinavian Riding Championships and winning second place! With another five years of hard work, she managed to qualify for Denmark's Olympic dressage team. Not only did she compete at the highest level possible, she proceeded to win silver at the 1952 Olympic Games in Helsinki. The gold-medal winner, St Cyr of Sweden, was so impressed with her stunning achievement that he stepped down from the podium to assist her to her place next to him. Four years later, at the 1956 Olympics, she repeated the feat and won silver again. Lis Hartel's perseverance and success inspired greater effort in numerous countries to offer horseback riding to people with disabilities.

Resources

Many countries now have organizations which oversee safety and certification of professionals and therapeutic centers. National and International Conferences are organized every year. College and university degrees in areas such as equine sciences and therapeutic riding are also possible.

Most therapeutic riding centers need help to keep their lessons affordable for their students. They are able to offer this kind of therapy thanks to the many people who generously donate money or volunteer their time and effort. People enjoy staying involved with horse therapy, because they witness how horses, with patience and trust, are able to give their riders the motivation and confidence to overcome obstacles and make major improvements. At times, riders find that they surprise themselves with their achievements. All members of the team, volunteers as well as the instructor in charge, share the pride in every newfound ability.

Information about Lis Hartel came from the following book:

Bud Greenspan, *100 Greatest Moments in Olympic History* (Special Centennial Ed. Santa Monica CA: General Publishing Group, Inc., 1995), page 26.

Websites and telephone numbers for more information about therapeutic horseback riding:

North American Riding for the Handicapped Association, Inc. (NARHA)
PO Box 33150 Denver, CO 80233
http://narha.org
800-369-RIDE (7433)

Certified Horsemanship Association (CHA)
5318 Old Bullard Road, Tyler, TX 75703
http://www.cha-ahse.org
800-399-0138

Special Olympics
1133 19th Street, N.W., Washington, DC 20036
http://www.specialolympics.org
800-700-8585

United States Paralympics
One Olympic Plaza, Colorado Springs, CO 80909
http://www.usparalympics.org
719-866-2030

Author Question and Answer

What inspired you to write this book?

I decided to write the first version of *Invincible* late one night in the winter of 2000 when I received a moving email from Lewis Kessler, one of my dear friends from law school. Lewis and his wife, Tamara, had taken their four-year-old identical twin daughters, Isabel and Olivia, to a remote location in Northern Poland where they had identified an unique (at the time) physical therapy program for Isabel who has cerebral palsy.* This was the family's fourth month-long journey to this location; the goal was to provide Isabel with an intense and individualized physical therapy program that would advance her physical abilities. That winter, Isabel was striving to take steps with the aid of crutches.

Lewis' email that night described Isabel's brute-strong, masculine physical therapist sobbing as he witnessed Isabel's extraordinary determination, stamina and will. This Russian therapist nicknamed Isabel, "My Pocket Hercules." That was the title of the first version of *Invincible*.

Lewis and Tamara's emails from their trips touched me deeply; I counseled them to retain the text of these writings as I saw them as the foundation of a book. After I read Lewis' email about the "Pocket Hercules," my reply said, "Do what you wish with your emails...I am writing a book."

That moment I determined to write a piece of popular fiction that would build a bridge between able-bodied and

---

*Cerebral palsy (CP) is a neuromuscular condition that usually onsets at birth. When someone has CP, messages from the brain to the muscles can get scrambled. So, although a person with CP knows what he/she wants his/her muscles to do, the muscle won't respond as intended because the instruction for its movement doesn't arrive properly. The severity of impairment can vary tremendously from person to person.

disabled children. I have so admired Olivia, along with Isabel, for she models how the able-bodied and disabled can enhance and nourish one another's lives. While in Poland, Olivia played with children of all ages and abilities. My impression from Lewis and Tamara was that Olivia effortlessly uncovered ways to genuinely interact with everyone. Today, at age 10, Olivia plays in a wheelchair basketball league with Isabel—because she can and because it enriches her.

As a family, the Kesslers have triumphed over physicians' early cautions that Isabel would face nearly insurmountable cognitive and physical challenges. Isabel is one of the sharpest young minds I have met and she has grown to take independent steps, while still spending most of her time on crutches or in a wheelchair. She also participates in therapeutic horseback riding. I believe Isabel's triumph belongs to the entire family, and notably Isabel's parents and grandparents, who have worked tirelessly and lovingly to buttress one another. The work is endless. As Isabel matures she faces new social and physical challenges—and these naturally impact the entire family system.

As I have nurtured this work, I have felt compelled to create a piece that might help influence a culture that not only is considerate of people with disabilities, but is poised to learn and grow from interactions with them. I want to help build a society that honors and respects everyone's humanity and thrives on our relationships with one another. Who better to target this message to then our children?

How long did you work on this book?

Four years of writing and editing, two more years until publication.

How many drafts did you write?

I don't even know. Early versions of this book were picture books. Working titles of various drafts included, *My Pocket Hercules, To Love Just the Same, Izka and O's Freedom Ride,* and *The Magic Spring.* Without those earlier versions, I would never have the work I have today. The heart of the story stayed the same, but the story line changed dramatically over the years of revision—and each revision was the foundation for the next.

At one point, I had a draft that I thought was worth sending to prospective publishers. I did send it to two publishers and received two rejections. Shortly thereafter, I attended a children's writer's conference and realized that I still had a considerable amount of work to do on the book. A friend suggested that I hire a professional editor. Hiring Melinda Rice as my editor was invaluable. She understood the heart of my book instantly, but also saw that I needed to rewrite extensively. The first comments she gave me must have been 7 pages long, single spaced. My heart dropped. I took a deep breath and read through them. I agreed with every single comment and went back to work. I completely rewrote the novel, cover to cover, twice with Melinda. The result is this book.

What was the most dramatic change in the plot over your many drafts?

In the earliest versions, there was no magical body of water at all. I added what was at first the Magic Spring in my effort to create a popular interest. When the magical water first appeared, the magic was triggered for anyone who had lived through 10 years, or a decade. Thus, the characters were nine years old at the book's outset and grew to 10 over the course of the book. When my editor strongly suggested that the princesses be older so as to appeal to a broader group of the

160

8–12 year old middle-grade novel target audience, I worried how I would create a trigger for the pond's magic. It didn't take long before I realized that the number 11 was a palindrome. I rushed to the Internet and rapidly uncovered a goldmine of metaphors and seeds for many new dimensions to the novel if my characters were 10 at the novel's outset and became 11 when they went to the pond. I believe that this somewhat accidental shift in the plot was the key to the novel achieving the popular flavor I had been looking for all along.

Acknowledgements

My name may have a prominent place on *Invincible's* cover, but, many others deserve attribution; without their input, this work would not exist. I have always been a proponent of collaboration because I genuinely thrive on connecting with others and because I am certain that collaboration breeds a better result. I hope that by including my contributors on this page they will understand, to some measure, my deep gratitude:

Mary Quattlebaum, my writing teacher, who exemplifies constructive criticism and who artfully nurtures all of her students' potential. Also, all of my writing classmates over the years who lovingly fostered the beginnings of this book.

Melinda Rice, my editor, who brilliantly and constructively guided me to reinvent the book and polish it for public consumption.

Margot Ott, dear friend and talented illustrator, who connected instantly with this work and brought it to life beyond my dreams.

Jeff Hunt and Isabel Kessler, whom I observed during therapeutic horseback riding lessons. The National Center for Therapeutic Riding, especially Robin Watts, and the Rock Creek Therapeutic Riding Center who allowed me to observe and ask questions. Nicoline Beveridge, therapeutic riding instructor extraordinaire and generous consultant to me on all horse details, and the author of the therapeutic riding afterword to this book. Caroline Springer, dear friend and advisor on all horse details and who spent a wonderful plane flight with me conjuring up Invincible's heroic survival of the storm.

Young readers: Emily and Molly Bernstein, Allie and Will Feldman, Sophie Steinman-Gordon, Julia, Shana and Elyse

Hausman, Annie Hills, Emily and Stephen Hutson, Kate James, Janie Macklin, Claire Romansky, Matthew Romansky, Francis and Zachary Rosenberg, Maddie Ross, Allison Vise, Lucas and Olivia Weals, Nathalie and Ben Gastevich.

Not so young readers, commenters, and phenomenal supporters: Sally Amoruso, Kathy Breitowich, Shirley Brandman, Cathy Nardi Gastevich, Lyndsey Van Vliet Gerber, Rich Greenberg, Amy Hancock, Alison and Ezra Hausman, Vicki Hutson, Jodi Macklin, Jill Meister, Suzi Nielsen, Jalene Spain, Jill Romansky McCulloch, Katie Romansky, Kira Romansky, Mike Romansky, Ady and Harry Rosenberg, Harry B. Rosenberg, Jr, Rachel Dvorken, Ralph Rosenberg and Uncle Ira Cohen.

David Ware, extraordinary friend and literary consultant, who immersed himself in my work with the careful and thoughtful attention he brings to all endeavors and who was essential to fleshing out my story lines.

Lucy Waletzky, dear friend and inspiration, who models a society that embraces and cherishes all people, regardless of their physical and/or cognitive abilities.

All my family members for their faith; most especially my nephew, Zachary Rosenberg and my stepdaughter, Katie Romansky, for supporting me every step of the way; and my son, Matthew, who had the brilliant idea that I publish the book through Imagination Stage. Joey, Jill, Matt, Kira and Fran —you also bolster me, and I am daily grateful.

Mark Williams who was the first disinterested party to embrace my vision and who inspired me to bring the work to a new level and to the public.

Linda Steinman, dear friend and law school roommate, who patiently waited for my publishable product and offered her wisdom and learned advice on the ways of the publishing world.

Liz Cutler, lifelong friend, teacher, mother of a disabled son, who thoughtfully reviewed this book and recommended adding an author interview for the benefit of teachers and students.

My Still Small Voice group for encouraging me to articulate what I really want in life and to make that happen. Publishing this book was a central item on my "I Want" list. Also, the "life purpose" element of this book derives from my studies with you.

Susan Toffler, Debra and Rich James, my fabulous friends and superior publicity team who guided me generously and expertly on promoting this book. Many other friends whom I anticipate will help me with their ties to journalists, media personnel, schools, etc...I thank you in advance and you will know who you are!

Tricia Brooks, Michael Manganiello, and Joe Canose, all of the Christopher Reeve Foundation, who generously embraced this work and offered their full support and assistance. I treasure my and Imagination Stage's collaborations with the Christopher Reeve Foundation in ways I will never adequately be able to articulate.

Judy Woodruff, for lending her name to this project and for her inspiration as an accomplished woman who is devoted to her family and who exhibits exemplary grace and perseverance.

Wayne Dixon, Lori Jenkins and Cindi Hott of HBP who patiently guided me through the printing process and who created a final presentation of this book that is absolutely beautiful.

Lauren Ridenour who stepped in as my assistant to save me from the madness of organizing the distribution and bookkeeping of the final product.

Imagination Stage and everyone who works there for embracing me in your family and for modeling a culture that values and nurtures every soul. Most especially, I thank Bonnie Fogel, Carol Gulley, Lisa Agogliati, Donna Salamoff, Madeline Burke, Laurie Levy-Page, George Borababy, Jerry Morenoff, JJ Finkelstein, Robby Brewer and Janet Stanford for their support of me personally and for the special attention they have devoted to this project. Without you, this dream of mine would not have come to fruition in this ideal way. You provided me a fitting vehicle to publish this work and I am forever indebted to you. I cherish the time I spend with you and on behalf of Imagination Stage…along with writing this novel, it is the most rewarding and gratifying aspect of my life outside of my family.

Finally, my mother, Francine C. Rosenberg, who sadly is not alive to share in this new chapter of my life. She inspired so many of my life choices. Remarkably, she inspired my writing for children after she died. It was in the first weeks after Mom's death in 1985 that I began to write a children's book. I couldn't sleep and was mulling over the vast array of profound emotions I was experiencing in the aftermath of Mom's struggle with cancer and her death. I felt compelled to write a book for my then six-month-old son, Matthew, to help him learn to express his feelings as he grew up. That was the beginning of the most rewarding personal journey I have ever taken…to become a writer. My connection to the Christopher Reeve Foundation also is attributable posthumously to my mother. Maria Trozzi, a wonderful lecturer we hired to speak at the Francine C. Rosenberg Memorial Lecture Series in Chicago, introduced me to Dana Reeve after I told her about my work with Imagination Stage and my efforts to write this book. Mom, I miss you desperately and I thank you for continuing to guide and inspire me.

Tribute
Dana And Christopher Reeve

Dana and Christopher Reeve were, for me, real life ambassadors for acceptance, courage and love. The Reeves inspired many aspects of Lena and Meg and informed the ending of *Invincible* which models a world in which people of all types and abilities thrive in each other's midst.

I feel a hole in my heart at their loss. Chris died in October, 2004 and Dana died just one week ago today. While I never met Chris, I was infatuated with him from afar and in awe of him as he triumphed over his accident. I had the distinct privilege of having met Dana twice in the last year. She was a totally authentic woman of extraordinary grace, dignity, and warmth. Down to earth and embracing, I witnessed her astounding capacity to inspire others and to instill in everyone with whom she interfaced a profound sense of self-worth and possibility.

I am deeply honored that the Reeves are associated with this work. My sincerest hope is that *Invincible*, Princesses Lena and Meg, and the Kessler family will, in some measure, carry on where Dana and Chris left off.

Sally
3-13-06

Bibliography

Anderson, Mary Elizabeth. *Taking Cerebral Palsy to School* (JayJo Books, LLC 2000)

Calder, Kate. *Horseback Riding in Action* (Crabtree Publishing Company, 2001)

Greber, Erika. *A Chronotype of Revolution: The Palindrome from the Perspective of Cultural Semiotics.* University of Munich/ University of California Irvine. www.realchange.org/pal/semiotic.htm

Jim Kalb's Palindrome Connection. www.palindromes.org. February 29, 2004.

Morris, Desmond. *Horsewatching* (Crown Publishers, Inc. 1989)

Presnall, Judith Janda. *Animals with Jobs, Horse Therapists* (KidHaven Press, 2002)

Wow, a Palindrome. Say the Same Forward and Backward—I Did, Did I? The Washington Post, March 1, 2004, at C15.